Finding Boaz

by
Izzy James

Published by Elizabeth C. Hull

Bent Knee Press

Published in the United States of America

First e-book edition: October 2014

First print edition: August 2016

ISBN: 978-0985229146

For my Jim who still believes in his Elizabeth

Chapter 1

"It's ten o'clock at night. What do you want?"

Abby Ericksen was looking through the screened door at her ex-husband, Brad. His breath was fogging up the glass in the top of the door. The cold March air swirled past her knees through the screen in the bottom of the door and began to freeze her tiny cube of an apartment.

There goes the budget, she thought.

"Won't you let me in?" he pleaded. He never did like the cold.

"Where's Suzie?" The door stayed locked between them.

"She left me. Please let me in. It's cold out here."

"What do you mean 'left'?" Ordinarily she would have let a poor body in from the cold, but this particular body had left her and Chloe out in the cold when he left them for Suzie. So she would worry about the electric bill later. He could freeze.

"I just wanted to talk to you." He rested his arm on the doorjamb and leaned in as if there were no glass between them. The fog got worse.

"I just want to do the right thing here." He stepped away from the door and put his hands in the pockets of his jacket.

Her heart was banging as she opened the door. She used to dream of him coming back to her and Chloe. It was all so romantic in her fantasy: Brad arriving home in the middle of the night, ragged and torn from the violent struggle that it took to get back; sweeping her off her feet; finally carrying her away to Neverland or some such place. But that was a year and a half ago, and she had given up those kinds of dreams.

Now that he was actually here, all she felt was anger and distrust. He stepped inside and leaned against the counter next to the back door. There were no signs of struggle. His blue Izod was completely intact under a black leather jacket that made her blue jeans and grandfather's old dress shirt feel frumpy.

Well, the time away from her had been prosperous for him anyway, she thought.

Crossing the ten-foot room, Abby backed up to the counter and got as far away from him as possible.

"I miss you, Ab, and I miss Chloe. I believe that we should be together. It's the right thing to do, don't you think?"

"I think you have a lotta nerve showing up here at my house in the middle of the night unannounced when I haven't seen you in eighteen months. That's what I think. So, what do you mean she left?" She crossed her arms over her chest.

"Can we stop talking about Suzie for a minute?"

"Don't you think she's relevant?"

"God allows these things for a reason, Ab, and I think that maybe we should just, you know, accept it." He opened his arms wide and started for her side of the room.

Abby sidestepped to the sink to clean up the tea glass she had sitting in it. What had he ever done but tout "what God said" and do the opposite? He came up behind her and put his hands on her waist. She felt giddy, like she might laugh, but it wasn't joy. Something wasn't right.

"Don't." She pushed him away.

He leaned against the counter next to her.

Stay in control, she thought. Abby turned to face him again. Beyond him she saw Chloe walk into the room.

"Momma?" Chloe's voice cracked with sleep. Brad turned in time to see her eyes widen.

"Daddy!" She ran and jumped into his arms.

"Hello, Chloe." Brad picked her up and held her close, but his eyes never left Abby. He sat down in a chair with the child on his lap. Chloe sat there quietly, almost sleeping. Abby leaned back against the sink with crossed arms. Maybe he was sincere. If so, it was the first time in at least eighteen months, although the timeline of his betrayal was much longer than that. Just then a brown spider scurried across the counter. She grabbed a paper towel and cleaned away the intruder.

"OK, Chloe, it's time to go back to bed." Abby retrieved her baby from his arms and carried her back to her room. She pulled the covers over the three-year-old tucking them around her tightly.

"Is Daddy staying with us, Momma?" Brad's eyes looked at her from the small face of her daughter.

"No."

When she returned, Brad was still sitting at the table. Abby took a seat across from him.

"What's all this?" He picked up one of the flyers lying amidst an organizational reorganization in the middle of the table. "Old Thyme Festival? So you're still into that music thing, huh?" His mouth curled into a smirk.

"Yep." She straightened the piles into two stacks and drew them to her side of the table.

"I wonder how you have time to do that and work and take good care of Chloe," he said.

"Oh, Chloe loved it."

"So you brought her with you?"

"Of course—Mom came to help. She had a blast." He was doing it again, insinuating that she wasn't good enough. Anger surged as she realized she was reacting in the same old way she always did with him—always explaining, trying to justify herself to him.

"Well, what do you think?" he asked.

"About what?"

"Do you want to give it another try? For Chloe's sake?" His eyes were pleading.

"I have to think about it," she said aloud, surprised to hear herself say anything that would give him the slightest hope.

He pulled out a business card with his name imprinted on one side; on the other side he had written in the phone numbers of the hotel where he was staying and handed it to her. Abby took the card and laid it on the table between them. She had forgotten what ugly hands he had. They were too small and white, delicate like a woman's.

"This is where I'll be. I'm transferring here. I'll be here for two weeks looking for a place to live. Would you like to have dinner tomorrow night?"

"I don't know. I have to think about it." She looked away from his gaze.

"About dinner? You have to think about dinner?" He made a little laugh as his mouth curled into that smirk again. "Look, I just want to take you and my little girl out for a meal, OK?"

"It's probably OK. Just call me tomorrow."

As soon as he was gone, she threw all the locks on the door and sat back down in her chair exhausted.

He wants me back?

There was no question about that. The mere thought made her sick. *I should have just said "no."* She swiped her hand into the air, a gesture of finality. "No."

Frustrated, Abby marched up and down the short length of the room. *What about Chloe?*

"How could he just show up here out of the blue like that?" she asked aloud.

The room was silent. Her dulcimer stood on its stand in the corner of the small living room. She closed Chloe's door and sat on the couch to play. Perhaps then she could sort out what she should do next.

The dulcimer sat comfortably in her lap. She put her music aside thinking to play unaided and free. At first she couldn't feel any rhythm, but after a few minutes, music began to fill the air. Her soul pulsed in time with the music she made, and it soothed her rattled nerves. She floated freely from one song to the next losing her worries to the phrases and refrains as she sang.

"Tom Dooley"... She had been playing "Tom Dooley" the day she first thought something was going on between Brad and Suzie.

The sun had been high and hot on the Fourth of July two years ago. Neighbors and friends had turned out for the annual block party. That year the buzz question had been whether or not Eddy Mullen would shoot a bottle rocket into a cop car as he had done the year before. Abby had been jamming with Joe Smith and his wife, Joan, on a makeshift stage on the Mullen's front porch. Brad carried Chloe on his hip making tours of the food tables. Generally Abby kept her eyes down on the fretboard or on her music when she was playing. If she didn't, she couldn't go very fast and Joe was lightning on the banjo. But she knew "Tom Dooley" inside and out, and she was feeling free and easy, no pressure, just playing with friends. When she looked up, she saw Brad hand Suzie something. Suzie wrapped her hands around his as she took whatever it was from him.

Abby looked down quickly. She couldn't hear the music, and she wasn't sure where she was in the piece. It took a second to realize she hadn't stumbled; her hands had kept the pace. She glanced once more to catch Suzie's look of triumph. Brad melted back into the crowd with Chloe.

"Poor boy, you're bound to die..."

She let the dulcimer ring the last notes until it rested quietly.

"Amazing grace! How sweet the sound."

Abby played the old song slowly, purely, letting the lonesome sound resonate.

Two days later, Brad was gone. Near as she could figure, the "something" she had seen was a set of keys and a lease. He and Suzie moved into an apartment across town and wouldn't tell her where. Brad came to see Chloe a couple of times, but Abby never saw Suzie again. Perhaps she was hiding out, ashamed to show her treacherous face to her friend.

After they were divorced and sold the house, Abby moved to Ocean View, not because she grew up there, but because it was where her mother lived. Abby had not realized that she missed the sea until she moved back within sight of its shores. The ever-present bigness of it had always helped her keep perspective on the size of her own troubles, and the constant splash and roar of the waves brought solace.

As Ocean View had grown to be her home, her mother had grown to be her friend.

There had been so many battles when she was younger, a whole five years ago, she chuckled to herself.

"'Tis grace that brought me safe this far..."

Her mother had been opposed to everything that Abby had tried after high school. When she found the Lord and a church, her mother had violently protested. So when Helen hadn't liked Brad, Abby wasn't surprised. She had attributed her mother's resistance to Brad as part of her general cynicism and overall dislike of people as a rule. Abby now understood that as an emergency room nurse, Helen had seen a lot of the bad side of humanity, and as a result, she had come to expect the worst of everyone.

At the time, Abby hadn't understood her mother's concerns. Abby saw the world through new eyes, and trusted everything and everyone. Her mother had been suspect of everything and everyone, and she had been so right.

The divorce had taken a full year to become final. The contact between her and Brad had been minimal. Chloe had never been an issue with him— Abby wanted her, Abby could have her. Chloe would be better off that way, he said. It made this present offer even stranger. She wondered if it would have been different if Chloe had been a boy.

"Did you ever hear tell of Sweet Betsy from Pike, who crossed the wide prairies with her lover Ike?" She played the old waltz quickly.

And now here he was.

She stopped playing.

She should just say, "No." Just no.

It would be so much easier to have help with Chloe, she argued with herself. Brad was her father after all; he should be helping with the child. It could be good for Chloe. She needed to have a father, and her own was probably the best bet to do a good job with her. And it would be so much easier to get by on more than just her income, which she thought wryly, she had no more as of today.

Imagine Stanley, her boss, a man at least thirty years older than her, thinking she'd take a boat ride with him, his friend, and a case of beer! Her stomach knotted as she remembered the twinkle in the older man's eye and the feel of his rough fingers on her forearm. She had said no, and walked out. Unemployed.

Could Brad be right? Did the Lord send him because of this present trouble? It wouldn't be the first time God had chosen an unbeliever to bring about His will.

Technically, Brad wasn't an unbeliever, she guessed, but he had gotten so good at manipulating the truth that she no longer knew if he really was saved. There had been a time when she was sure of it, but no more.

Abby began to play the waltz again. *Well, what about Chloe*, she asked herself. If he's decided to act like her father then it might be good for her. He can have visitation. She stopped short. *Would he steal her?*

Not likely. If he had wanted her so badly, why would he have dumped her in the first place and not seen her in eighteen months?

She began to play again.

I just won't let him see her alone. If he wants to see her, he'll just have to see me too.

Her thoughts turned to her interview on Monday. Perhaps that was what God had in store for them next. The idea of working for a company of charter boats intrigued her. There was romance in the thought of pirate ships and being free on the waves in the light of the moon, the friendly beacons of lighthouses and brisk breezes....

Right, I'll likely freeze my knees. She laughed.

Of course, it might just be great.

"And Betsy, well satisfied, said with a shout, 'Good-bye, you big lummox, I'm glad you backed out.'"

Abby finished the song with a flourish. After she returned the dulcimer to its stand, she stood and stretched. The peace she felt radiated to her fingers and toes. She was ready for bed.

All that was left was to tell Brad.

Chapter 2

Duncan MacLeod sat at the head of the large, brilliantly shined dining room table. His mother sat at the opposite end. His brothers, all four of them, were evenly divided on the sides. The tinkling of her spoon on the crystal glass brought their attention to her. She stood.

"Duncan, I wish to address you now," she said in her most formal tone. They hushed. Erin MacLeod was still quite beautiful standing amidst the candlelight and crystal. Her face had thinned from grief, the lines of laughter had deepened, but her hair still shown a dark, glossy black and her green eyes were still clear and bright.

"Yes," Duncan answered.

He knew what was about to come: the official transfer of power from oldest son to head of the family. His father, Lachlan, had been dead for three months. Duncan had assumed command of MacLeod Enterprises as he had been trained, but the official ceremony had not taken place. Now they were all here, dressed in their clan's tartan, to participate in his family's ancient rite of transfer.

"Duncan, you are the first born," Erin continued in a loud, clear voice.

A servant moved around them quietly filling six ceremonial glasses with a dark liquid. Each head of clan MacLeod had taken his first drink from these glasses since the first Duncan MacLeod, newly immigrated to America, had purchased them for the rite of his son, Lachlan.

"It falls then to you to be our leader. Are you aware of all that this requires?" Erin went on.

Duncan sat straighter in his chair wondering if he should stand. He felt as if his forebears stood around him in unison, with glasses raised, waiting.

"I do," he said.

"Do you agree to abide by the laws of God and this land and of the MacLeods?"

"I do."

"Do you"—she looked with pride around the table at her boys, now grown men— "children of MacLeod, accept this Duncan as your new leader, and accede to him all the rights and privileges that befit the Chief of the MacLeods?"

"We do," they answered in unison.

Erin MacLeod raised her glass, and her sons followed suit.

"Stand and raise your glasses to hail the new MacLeod." They all stood and lifted their glasses. The whiskey glowed amber in the soft light.

"Hail, MacLeod!"

As they drank, Duncan stood and joined them.

"Thank you" he said.

They sat back down, for they had just begun.

Each of his brothers had prepared a speech to declare his loyalty to him and to their family.

Angus was next in age to Duncan, so he was next to stand and raise his glass. A giant of a man, he had to be careful not to bang his glass on the chandelier.

"Duncan, I'll work for you as I worked for our father. I pledge you my loyalty."

He reminded Duncan of the huge ancient warriors of centuries past. He was intelligent, and he could have wielded a broadsword without any difficulty. His work on their fleet of boats was invaluable. Angus had been their Dad's right-hand man, the leader in Duncan's absence, working side by side with their father. Duncan had come home to the States one year ago, but had only come home to stay four months before tonight.

As Angus sat down, Douglas stood. Douglas was a tall man though shorter than Angus and darker than his brothers. He reminded Duncan of his mother's family. Fresh out of law school, Douglas did not work for MacLeod holdings.

"Duncan MacLeod, I hereby declare my undying allegiance and faithfulness to you." He drank from his glass. "Of course, if you ever need a lawyer..."

Duncan laughed and shook his brother's hand. Douglas sat back down again.

"To Duncan, the one worthy to lead us all to greatness." Andrew was composing a new song, Duncan guessed. "You are my master, dear brother." He bowed with a flourish.

"Thank you, I think." Laughter rumbled through the room.

Finally, it was time for Geordie, the baby. He

was doing quite well in his second year at Ocean View Technology. Computers had captured his mind and future.

"Duncan, I don't know what to say...um...good job, and I'll follow wherever you lead us...you know, loyalty and all that stuff." Duncan stood to meet him and shake his hand as well.

"Thank you, Geordie."

Duncan felt sheepish as he accepted their praise, but his heart swelled with thankfulness. He hadn't felt this good when he finished the Special Forces Qualification Course and was permitted to don his green beret.

When his brothers were finished, Erin stood and brought to him a large old book.

"These are the Chronicles of MacLeod. In them you will find the rules we live by and the deeds we have done. They are for you to continue. May the Lord of our fathers always bless you and keep you."

"The Lord bless you and keep you!" the brothers chimed in, and they drank again.

Duncan accepted the book from her hand. It was bound in leather, heavy and tough, not crumbly as he had anticipated. He need not fear opening and reading the old stories.

As Erin returned to her place, Duncan had a mystical feeling that nothing would now ever be the same.

"Mother." He looked at her and stood. Raising his glass, he said, "Erin Maureen Dalrymple MacLeod." She smiled at him. "You have done your duty with honor and courage. May you live your life long and full with a house filled with grandchildren and great-grandchildren and great-great-grandchildren at your knees."

"To Erin MacLeod!"

They all drank. The formalities over, Duncan slouched into his chair and talk took over as dinner was served.

"So, Duncan, when are you gonna start giving Mom all those grandchildren at her knees?" asked Geordie.

"He can't until he's married," said Andrew.

"And he can't get married until some girl asks him," said Douglas.

"I don't think I'd want a girl brazen enough to ask me to marry," Angus said.

"Very funny." Duncan had forgotten about the marriage rule. Somewhere in the back of his mind was the story of how his father wooed his mother, but he had forgotten the details. Oh well, there would be time to catch up on that stuff later. It was probably written in the Chronicles. He was looking forward to the book, and his brothers probably got it wrong anyway. And now they had other business to discuss.

He had decided to tell them of their father's plans tonight. He and Lachlan had been working on this one longer than any of them knew. Lachlan had hoped to tell them himself, but his death had put a stop to many plans.

It was risky; it would take most of their capital, but it was worth a try. As the fishing dried up, something had to replace it, and Lachlan had looked hard for something to guard the family fortunes. Lachlan's answer was charter boats— rentable recreational boats on the Bay—that would travel the Delmarva Loop. True, it wasn't rocket science, but it wasn't being done yet either.

He wasn't keen to tell them of their new

venture. Dougie, the lawyer, liked to argue, and play devil's advocate. He was ready for that. The real key was Angus. He had worked side by side with their father while Duncan was gone on active duty in the Army. If Angus was against him, the others would follow. He was prepared to pull rank, but he hoped it wouldn't come to that yet. Angus didn't like change.

"Listen, guys, I have something to tell you. I have a new idea to expand our present operations." His brothers gave him their attention as he described the broadening of their operations to include two new vessels that would provide trips to Tangier Island out in the middle of the Chesapeake Bay. These were to be overnight trips that included passenger participation. Eventually they would expand even farther out into the Atlantic.

His brothers were silent. Angus looked at his hands before him on the table. Dougie's eyes were bulging and his face was flush. Andrew sat back with arms across his chest glaring at no one in particular. Geordie looked excited.

"The liability is tremendous! Did you think of that?" Douglas exploded.

"Yes, Douglas, Dad and I both thought of that. We will get the appropriate coverage, and the boats we picked are very stable. We want adventure, not lawsuits."

"I don't know, Duncan. It sounds risky."

"What kind of life would we live without risks, Doug?"

Angus was silent; he needed the time to put it together. Duncan could wait.

"Andrew?"

"I don't know why you have to change things.

Why can't it stay the same? We are doin' all right as it is."

"Because the world is changing, Andy. The fish aren't what they once were, so we need to expand. There's a market, and we should seize it." His father's words came out of him as if he had rehearsed them. He had the same fears when Lachlan had first proposed the plan to him.

"What if we fail? What if we lose everything?"

"We aren't risking everything, so we can't lose everything," Duncan replied.

Andrew remained sitting with his arms crossed, glaring at Duncan. *It will just take some time.* Lachlan's words reassured him from the past.

"When do we start?" Geordie could barely contain his excitement.

"The first boat has already been ordered. It will be here later in the month. We'll hire someone to do the grand opening and invite all the travel agents from D.C. to Richmond, even down to Norfolk." Angus looked up from his hands to engage Duncan.

"Angus?"

"I'll work for you as I worked for our father. I don't see that he was wrong, and I'm willing to bet on you." Duncan was relieved. The conversation turned to boats and routes and liability forms. The business of eating took over, and by the time dinner was over Duncan was satisfied that he and his brothers were once again a team.

After dinner, Duncan left the table but stopped to kiss his mother on the cheek and pick up the book of Chronicles as he went to his office. He needed to brush up on these rules. He'd forgotten that one about marriage and he wondered how many others there were. He'd been away in the

Army a good while. Some of those stories he hadn't heard since he was a kid.

The wood paneled office that used to be his father's was now his. It contained a solemnity and peace that scared him as a child. Now its ambience comforted him. His father's things were still there: books and charts, his sextant, his desk. He could feel the strength of his dad in this room. The rest of the house had the softer feel of his mother.

He placed the book down on the desk. It had lived in this room longer than he had been alive. He sat down behind the sturdy wooden desk, pulled the big book to him and began to thumb through the pages. His eye fell on a list of rules set up by the Laird of MacLeod in 1735.

"These rules are to be a covenant between our people and us, the Lairds of MacLeod. Follow them and prosper; ignore them and be cursed. Lose thy land and thy fortune, thy bride and all that thou hast claim to except thy mortal soul which thou may give to God if ye so choose."

"Measure justice with an even hand. Ye may not give preference to the poor man because he is poor, nor to the mighty man because of his might, nor to the rich man because of his wealth. Ye must judge righteously between neighbors."

Duncan scanned down the page further, through various punishments for stealing and other offenses.

"Each chief, if not already wed, must choose a wife and not six months out, to bear thee children and so gain thee wisdom to lead. Thou mayest not ask a woman to wed

with thee. She must ask thee. This will ensure thy happiness. Thou mayest not divorce."

Duncan slapped the book closed. What were they thinking? Is this supposed to be funny? He could almost hear the laughter of Duncan, the first Laird of MacLeod, down through the ages. He looked up to see his mother standing in the doorway.

"You were meant to be in this room at this time, Duncan."

"Mom, they had to be kidding about this marriage stuff. This was hundreds of years ago. We don't do things like this anymore. I can't imagine where I will find someone to ask me to marry in six months. These days people just move in together and try it out for a few years first."

"Do you remember the story of Diggory MacLeod?"

"No—and that's the other thing, I haven't heard some of these stories since I was a kid."

As Duncan's frustration mounted, he began to pace the floor. Erin strode into the room and leaned on the corner of the old desk.

"Diggory MacLeod was a new laird of MacLeod at the turn of the last century. He thought he would change things. After all, it was a new century and things were changing. So he waited seven months and asked the girl himself. He lost it all. His wife was barren, and he died a young man and a very poor one as well. His brother, your grandfather, was next in line and became chief. He went back to the old ways. He built a fortune and passed it to your father who built this business and the wealth that we have. Your father stuck to the old ways because they work."

"So why didn't they kick him out?"

"Because he was the chief. If he prospers, the family prospers. If he doesn't, it doesn't. He wasn't a criminal, Duncan."

Duncan continued pacing. It was impossible.

"So basically I have to meet a girl, or maybe I already know one, and get her to ask me to marry her. In six months." He stopped to face Erin.

"Be careful, Duncan. You want someone to love you and marry you. Not just marry all this." Erin waved her hand around the room.

Chapter 3

Just before she woke, the fog of sleep cleared and Abby saw herself standing in a boat with large white sails. The boat was afloat on a clear green sea. The wind surrounded her body as she followed a large white storm. She woke up after that and lay wondering what it could mean. After an hour, she gave up on sleep and went to the kitchen.

The warm smell of coffee comforted her as she sat down with her Bible at the kitchen table. She had an hour before Chloe would be awake and take over her day. She rested her head on her hands.

Brad.

She felt an adrenaline surge and shifted back and forth in her seat. The thought of confrontation sent spirals of tension through her stomach.

Someone knocked at the door. Abby nearly came out of her skin.

She stood up and tiptoed over to the door hoping that it wasn't Brad stopping by unannounced. Instead, her mother was standing there juggling a brown bag and a casserole dish.

She slipped the door open quietly.

"What are you doing here?" she asked in an urgent whisper hoping not to wake Chloe.

"Good morning to you, too." Her mom barged past her and practically dropped the casserole dish onto the counter.

"This is the taco salad you asked me to make for that church thing you have today. And these are bagels for breakfast. I smell the coffee." She helped herself to a cup and sat down at the table.

Abby grinned with relief.

"Gosh, I forgot all about that. Thank God."

"You forgot about the social that you asked me to cook for? And bring over here before my shift?"

"Sorry." Abby set out knives, cream cheese, and plates and took a seat across from her mother.

"You won't believe who showed up here last night."

"Who?" Her mother's eyes filled with alarm.

"Brad." Abby watched the fear in her mom's eyes turn back to the usual cynicism.

"What'd he want?" She brought the coffee to her mouth.

"He says he wants me and Chloe back."

Her mom stilled. Then she asked, "What are you going to do?"

Abby was surprised at her mother's reserved tone. As a rule, she was quick with an opinion.

"I don't want him. But he can have visitation with Chloe if he wants," Abby said.

"I would trust him as far as I could throw him." She shook her bagel at Abby. "Don't let Chloe go out with him alone."

"Why?"

It was odd to have her mother confirm what she had already felt.

"I don't know. I just don't like it."

"Yeah, me either, but at least I have the church social, so I have a way out of dinner with him tonight. I wish you would come to the social with me."

"You already know I have to work, and besides, that's not my thing." She sipped her coffee. "You know you should get out and get a life."

"I have a life, Mama. Her name is Chloe." It was the same conversation they had shared many times before. The only change was who started it.

"Yes, I know, but it's not good for you to be alone all the time with no one but your old mother for company. You need a man."

"You don't have a man, Mom, and you're not old."

"Yes, that's true..." She paused for another bite. "And I do like men... I just don't want to live with any more of 'em. But you're different. Chloe could use a daddy, and then you would be safe here, and I wouldn't be afraid for you all the time."

"I'll get a dog." They laughed together.

"Seriously, Mama, I don't pick men well. But dogs—now that's different. I might have a fighting chance with a dog, and even a return policy." She grinned and they laughed again. This time they woke Chloe, and she came out of her room and planted herself in her grandma's lap. Abby fixed her a bagel.

"You should do like what Aunt Mae said," Helen went on. "She figured that if she only went out with rich men, then she would only fall in love with a rich man."

Abby's face must have looked as if she didn't get it because her mom continued to explain.

"Don't use your heart; use your head. Keep your eyes and ears open. Research, you know, like those arranged marriages in the olden days. Pick a good man, and you can learn to love him. You could make a list." She smiled.

"Make a list? I'll have to think about that one."

"Well, baby," Helen said to Chloe still curled up in her lap, "I gotta go to work."

The cold wind from the night before had brought in mild weather for the day. Not an unusual thing for spring along the Virginia coast. Abby spent the rest of the day with Chloe catching up on the laundry and taking a short trip to the park. When Brad called, she begged off, telling him that she had to be at the church for the social for which she had volunteered. She made arrangements to see him on Monday evening after dinner.

Chapter 4

Duncan felt the still peace of the old sanctuary. The church, built in the eighteenth century, was converted to a non-denominational Christian fellowship a few years ago after sitting vacant for several years. Hundreds of people had prayed and celebrated here and the beams, the windows, the very air retained the memories. He took a deep breath. It was good to be home, and he would make this place his new church home.

The MacLeods had always attended a church across town, and he had gone with them until he left home. Somehow he had missed Jesus there. He found Jesus in a non-denominational church like this one when he was in the Army in Kentucky. His mother and brothers were content with their church, and so far, he was content to leave them there.

The sign outside had advertised a community social today, and he thought that was a good way to meet some of the people who attended.

Things had been moving quickly since he had become the MacLeod. Moving home again with its memories was not as tough as he thought it would be. No one had brought up that night ten years ago when he was forced to leave. Not even his brothers. Perhaps the trauma had healed in his absence.

He sat still, breathing deeply to allow the peace of the room to calm and restore some equilibrium to his soul. He closed his eyes. The new boat wasn't going to arrive on time, but he figured he would still have time to be up and running by the opening of the season. Everything else was coming together nicely. Except for a bride. Where was he going to find one and still do all the work necessary to launch the new division?

He opened his eyes and standing before him, at the front of the sanctuary, was a tiny woman, with her back to him, hands raised in quiet praise. He felt an electric current run through him. Her hair shown a deep chestnut and hung down to her waist in waves. She made no sound as she swayed. He began to feel like a peeping Tom, so he cleared his throat.

She spun around abruptly, as if someone had slapped her. A blush rose to her cheeks. The electric current pulled him to her. He stood, stepped out of the pew, and made his way to stand in front of her.

"I'm sorry, I—"

"Oh, no," she interrupted him, "it's OK. I just didn't know you were there."

Her voice was musical, gentle, and soft.

She turned her face upward to smile at him and stuck out her hand. "I'm Abby."

The sun caught her green eyes; Duncan caught his breath. He took her hand and was shaken.

"Duncan. I've just come home from the Army."

"Oh?" Abby gently pulled her hand away with a little pink color still in her cheeks. Just then a little girl came in squealing and careened directly into her backside. As she swung around again to catch the little girl, her hair brushed by him and he could smell roses.

"Mama! Mama! Can I go with Rachel? Can I? Can I?"

"Where is Miss Debbie?"

A short blonde woman burst through the door just then with a little blonde-haired girl in tow.

"Oh, Abby. I was scared to death. She just took off to find you and..." The woman stopped to breathe. "I'm going to take them outside to the swings."

"OK." Debbie stuck out her hand for Chloe, and Chloe ran to her. They were gone, and the sanctuary was quiet again

"That was my daughter, Chloe." Her face glowed with pride. "Have you met anyone yet? I'll be happy to introduce you to the pastor."

"Sure."

Was she married? He sneaked a look at her hand as he held the door open for her. She wore a gold ring on the middle finger of her left hand. What did that mean?

They passed through the double doors into a main hallway lined with windows, which in turn led to the parish house and classrooms. Through the windows, he could see people milling about outside on the lawn in the mild February day.

The sun was high in the sky at three in the afternoon, but by four thirty, he knew the sun would be setting. They found Pastor Bob without any difficulty because at six foot four inches tall, he was the tallest man in the room. He had bright white hair that glowed in the light coming from the windows behind him. He was standing alone sipping from a Styrofoam cup.

"Pastor Bob, I would like to introduce..." She turned to Duncan.

"Duncan." He shook hands with the pastor.

"So are you a friend of Abby's?" he boomed and slipped an arm across her shoulders.

Abby flamed a most becoming bright red. Pastor Bob dropped his arm from her and Duncan watched her melt into the background as the preacher took over the hosting duties.

"No, sir, I'm new here...well, to this church. I come from Ocean View, but I've been away in the Army."

"Really. Well, we are glad to have you with us. Come on, let me introduce you around."

With that he plunged into the crowd. Duncan followed. He did manage to monitor Abby's progress as she made her way through the mass of people and through another set of double doors that led outside. Briefly, he made eye contact with a big blonde man who, he surmised, had also been watching Abby.

Chapter 5

The cool air of the last half of the day was refreshing after the stuffy heat of the parish hall. Abby took a deep breath as she hustled over to relieve Debbie.

"So, who's the hunk?" Debbie's eyebrows went up and down.

"I haven't heard that word since junior high school."

"OK, so who's the hunk?" Debbie, her best friend, was grinning now.

"I don't know. He's new to our church. His name is Duncan. I introduced him to the pastor, and that was that."

"I bet that was not just that. Did you see the way he looked at you?"

Abby had to admit that she had. She held her right hand in a fist to her chest; she imagined she could still feel the electric tingle his hand had given her and the warmth that had spread itself into desire. OK, Ab, remember: *head not heart* and certainly not anything else. *Research.*

Right.

She took a deep breath and placed her right hand on the cold steel pole of the swing to ground the charge she still felt. He's just another man. A dramatically handsome man. She couldn't argue with that or that her reaction to him had been strong—more than she had ever felt meeting any other man—but even still, he was just another man.

Right.

The parish hall had a small stage set up on one end of the room. The backdrop was a panel of windows overlooking a stand of trees dressed in gray, perfect for a winter snowfall. After a short welcome from Pastor Bob, the music began. Duncan was gratified to see Abby, who he had lost track of, up on the stage with a strange-looking instrument.

It was as shapely as the woman herself: an hourglass, long and slender. He had not ever reacted so strongly to a woman and certainly not since his vow of abstinence five years ago. Before that, he had been free to sow wild oats, and he had planted acres. But this time, it was different. He needed a wife, and you couldn't choose a wife on savage impulse.

Abby kept her eyes down as she played. The sunlight shining through the windows flashed on her hair as she strummed rapidly. He liked the bluegrass flavor of the song. He couldn't take his eyes off Abby. When she did look up, she looked right at him and then abruptly looked away. Attributing that to her need for concentration, he continued to stand mesmerized for the two songs she played. As she was leaving the stage area, he maneuvered around the crowd to intercept her at the door.

"What is that?" He pointed to the instrument.

"It's a mountain dulcimer." She didn't smile at him this time; she was busy looking around him for something or someone.

Then her face lit up. "Excuse me," she said and quickly brushed by him leaving a tantalizing whiff of roses.

Duncan hurried to the door. He couldn't let her leave until he had her phone number or some other way to get in touch with her. Once outside, he saw her dulcimer in a small yellow car. Chloe was running around on the grass.

Their eyes met when she closed the trunk. She stuck out her hand for Chloe as she stepped up onto the curb.

The two of them approached him together.

"Hello." She looked directly into his eyes, challenging him, sizing him up. He could see honesty and intelligence shining out from her olive green eyes.

Then her eyes twinkled.

"Wanna swing?"

His heart lurched. She was teasing him.

She let go of Chloe, and the little girl ran to the playground.

"OK," was the only word he could muster from the shock numbing his brain. *OK.*

They walked toward the play area together. In the bright light of the sun, as he walked next to Abby, he noticed that while her clothes were immaculate, there was tiny fraying on the collar of her dress. He saw no signs of wear in Chloe's clothes, which were sharp and stylish. Chloe grabbed the first swing she came to and climbed aboard the little seat. Abby took her place behind her and began to slowly push the giggling child.

"The pastor told me you ran the Old Thyme Festival last summer."

"Yes, I did. Do you like old time music?"

"I don't really know. I haven't heard much of it. I have heard a little bluegrass. Like Rocky Top."

"Not the same thing. Similar. But definitely not the same thing." She smiled at him and pushed Chloe.

"Are you married?" The words fell out of his mouth before he could edit them.

"No. You?"

It sounded like the challenge he had seen in her eyes.

"I wouldn't be here with you if I were."

Her eyes shot up to meet his own. The challenge still not satisfied.

"I'm glad to hear that," she said.

"Why?"

"Because not everyone acts that way." She appeared to be struggling with telling him more.

"Like who?"

"My boss. Yesterday he invited me for a boat ride. Him, his friend Jack or somebody, and me. They'd bring the beer. They weren't bringing their wives."

Anger surged from deep in Duncan's soul. He could understand any man finding Abby attractive. But if he ever met this boss, he'd take him out.

"What did you do?"

"I quit."

Chloe got off the swing and ran to the slide.

"But you know what I've found?" she continued. "That God always supplies what I need when I need it. You know the Word says that He is the husband to the widow and a father to the fatherless."

He nodded his response. He was familiar with the passages and he wanted her to keep talking.

"Earlier this week, a friend of mine told me about a position that was opening up in her company. So after I got home yesterday, I called her and made an appointment to be interviewed."

"Where?" He was feeling chills at the recognizable hand of God.

"MacLeod Tours." He was getting used to mind-numbing shock just as he was getting used to the rightness he felt about this woman.

"I hear they are a good company to work for," she went on. "Who knows, maybe I'll even get to go to sea one day."

"Do you want to go to sea?"

"Well..." She looked away up to the treetops this time. "It sounds like an adventure. To be free. But they only charter boats up and down the river, so the chances are slim." She laughed.

Duncan wondered what made her feel trapped enough to want to be free.

"So what about you?" She changed the subject and her focus. They watched a new green pickup truck pull into the parking lot. "Are you out of the Army or just home on leave?"

"Home for good. My dad died recently, and I've

inherited the family business."

"Oh, I am sorry." He believed her.

"Daddy!!!" Chloe's scream pierced his eardrums and she took off running.

"Excuse me." Abby left to follow. Chloe was picked up by the tall man and swung around. Abby stood back with her arms crossed. After the man had put Chloe on the ground, he spoke with Abby. Then she turned and waved a half-hearted good-bye to him. The man went to his truck. Abby strapped Chloe in the car and drove away following the man in the green truck.

How about that. Duncan walked out to his own car not wanting to go back into the throng of the well-meaning congregation. He had come looking for a little peace and quiet and what he got was a bundle of trouble in a beautiful brown-haired package. He wished he could do something to help her.

He admired her determination. She just lined up an interview and moved on. Duncan dug out his cell phone and dialed Angus. This was to be the first test of his power, and he hoped he wouldn't get an argument.

Duncan took a deep breath to steel himself. He had known a moment like this was coming, but he had hoped that his first request would be a little more reasonable to the ear.

"Angus, Monday there is a young woman coming for an interview. Her name is Abby. I don't know her last name. But I want you to hire her. I want her to have full benefits...anything she needs... medical... you know—the works." He took a breath. "And Angus, be helpful."

"What do you mean 'be helpful'?"

"I mean helpful. Show her where stuff is, introduce her around. Make her feel welcome. Make her some coffee."

"Would you like me to call in the boys and build a special wing for her tomorrow? It's Sunday, but I'm sure—"

"Enough. I'm serious, Angus." He hung up the phone.

It was a nice evening. Duncan decided to drive around and have a look at the town he missed so much when he was gone. It looked the same to him except for the new strip mall on the south end of town. It housed a video store, an exotic lingerie shop, a sub shop, and a frozen yogurt store. Duncan remembered his mother telling him about the controversy the lingerie shop caused when it opened. People from the surrounding neighborhoods protested with picket signs. It was a pretty lively event for the folks of Ocean View. Didn't stop the shop from moving in though.

Not far from there was the turnoff to the Gordon's old house. He found himself on the familiar street without making a conscious effort. A warm glow lit the plate glass window of the old bungalow. It had been his second home in childhood. He didn't linger long on the street; he knew he was no longer welcome.

As he continued to drive up and down the familiar streets, his thoughts returned to Abby. She had been so changeful—smiling at him and avoiding him, and then teasing him. His reaction to her teasing him about the swing was unsettling. His heart was going to be gone quickly if he wasn't careful.

Chapter 6

"How dare he show up here," Abby muttered to herself as she drove away. He never could take no for an answer. She'd gone with him to avoid a scene in front of Duncan.

She couldn't believe that she had just done that: gone off with a strange man, flirted with him, nearly told him all her dreams. What had she been thinking?

That was just it: she hadn't been thinking. She was drawn to him. She had never felt like that toward any man, not even Brad. Hadn't she just talked about that this morning with her mom? Butterflies returned when she thought of Duncan standing there in the sunlight. His sandy red hair glowed in the sun. His body was lean and squarely built with wide, full shoulders. He had worn a dark blue suit, with a curious yellow plaid handkerchief tucked in the pocket that complimented his coloring.

Abby turned the car into the fast-food restaurant and parked a couple of spaces away from

Brad's brand new truck. She hadn't seen it last night, and the sight of it now irritated her. *What else does he have? A new house, new sexy neighbors?*

Oh, God forgive me. Her prayer did nothing for the irritation of seeing him festering under her skin. She couldn't shake the idea that he was up to something. Brad was all smiles as he approached Chloe, who put her arms up to be carried. Abby followed the two of them into the red-topped building and up to the counter to order the kid's meal and two meals for him. They found a seat in the indoor play yard. Abby couldn't eat. Brad proceeded to wolf down his food like a troll. Chloe ate a couple of fries and went off to play in the ball pit.

"Well, have you made up your mind?"

She could barely make out the words around the wad of hamburger circling one side of his mouth.

"Yes."

His eyebrows shot up, and a grin began to spread across his face.

"No," she said quickly, "I have decided no. But you can see Chloe if you want ... according to our divorce agreement."

His face turned red. She watched the lump of meat slide down his throat like a snake digesting a mouse.

"Why?" His voice was quiet.

"I think we are better off. I don't want to change things. Except that I think it would be good for Chloe to see you sometimes." She folded her hands together in front of her on the table hoping to hide their shaking.

He stuffed a handful of fries into his mouth and chewed just enough to make room for a long swig of soda before crunching up the remains of his food into a paper ball. Then he swiveled around on the chair to face the playground and kept his back to Abby.

Abby looked at her watch and timed fifteen more minutes for Chloe to play. Then they would leave. During that time, Brad didn't look at her once.

Images of Duncan distracted her like a magic spell. The warmth and cheerfulness in his manner drew her to him. He was dangerously handsome. She could still see him standing there as she waved good-bye. He looked like a warrior, strong and still. She warmed to the possibilities. He seemed genuine. He had said that he would not have been with her if he was committed elsewhere, and for some inexplicable reason she felt that she could trust him.

Brad stood up and called her back to reality. She couldn't tell a dove from a snake.

Chapter 7

Abby loved church on Sundays. The church bells were bonging, the air was crisp and invigorating. The day was full of promise. Chloe was cute in her blue and white sailor dress with black patent leathers. Abby was wearing her grandfather's diamond chip tie clasp under the collar of her blouse. She had just gotten it back from the jeweler who had made it into a pin. It was the most valuable thing she owned.

Mrs. Young smiled at Chloe and patted her head; Abby looked around at the crowd. Maybe she would see Duncan.

Chloe couldn't wait to get to her three-year-old class to play with Rachel. Abby dropped her off and hurried to find a seat in the sanctuary.

She'd just plopped down when a man blocked the window and cast a shadow across her.

"May I sit here?" She looked up into Duncan's smiling face, and her heart skipped a beat.

"Of course." She scooted farther into the pew,

bumping elbows with Mrs. Petersen to make room for his large frame. Every pew was packed in the tiny church. That's why he chose to sit next to her, she told herself. His warm smile and twinkling eyes told her otherwise.

"I thought you'd be up there." Duncan pointed toward the front of the sanctuary where the worship team was gathering.

"I will be for Easter. With Chloe I can't always make practice, so I do it when I can."

After the service, Lars, her Sunday school leader, stopped in front of their pew. His smile showed every one of his pearl white teeth.

"Are you coming to the Singles brunch today?"

"Yep. I'm gonna drop Chloe off at Mom's first." She hoped it wasn't obvious that she didn't want to ride with him to the restaurant.

Abby turned to Duncan. "This is Lars. He is one of our Sunday school leaders. We are going to Sammy's for their breakfast bar. Would you care to join us?"

"Sure." Duncan smiled even broader than he did before.

"OK. Well, I'll see you there then." Lars moved on through the crowd.

Duncan got out of his car as Abby pulled into the parking lot of Sammy's. He was still grinning at her deft maneuver to get out of riding with Lars. He doubted that Lars was fooled, but she obviously thought she was letting him down easy. He liked that she was so careful about the man's feelings.

"You didn't have to wait for me."

"Well, other than Lars, I wouldn't know who to link up with, and I'm not sure he's here yet."

"Oh, well, come with me then."

Abby turned from him and led the way into the eatery without looking at him again. *Of course he wasn't waiting for you*, Abby cursed herself as she led Duncan into Sammy's. She spotted Lars at a long table with four members of their class. Mrs. Young and Mrs. Bennett, the oldest members, were in conversation with Lars. Mrs. Petersen, a good-looking woman in her early fifties, was chatting with Tammy, the youngest member, about something. Tammy stared at Duncan as he approached.

"Everyone, this is Duncan," Lars said. Abby, absorbed in observing Tammy, had not noticed Lars stand up.

After they introduced themselves, Patty, their waitress, appeared to take their order.

Everyone stood up and moved toward the breakfast bar.

Abby's stomach twisted. She was thankful she was not already married to this man. Her nerves couldn't take it. What if he hurt her? Perhaps she should add "ugly" to her list of requirements.

"Shall we go up to the bar?" Duncan asked.

Abby stood. Duncan's hand in the small of her back gently set her in the right direction. She stepped a little forward to remove the pleasant sensation.

Everyone was waiting for them to return so they could bless the food together. Tammy sat across from Duncan.

"So, Duncan, how long have you been here?"

Tammy's straight brown hair was nearly black and glittered in the sun from the window behind them. She took a bite while she listened to Duncan's answer.

"About a month. My father passed away."

"Ohh." Sincerity dripped from the clear blue eyes. "Did he know the Lord?"

"Yes, he did."

"You must really miss him. Were you close?"

"Yes, we were, and yes, I do miss him very much."

Abby was beginning to chafe under the realization that by the time breakfast was over Tammy would know more about him than she did. How could he resist someone so obviously interested in him? *Why do you care anyway?* she asked herself. *Remember head not heart.*

"How's your mother, Abby?" Lars smiled at her from the end of the table.

"She's OK. She made that taco salad everyone raved about yesterday."

"I had some of that. It was good."

"I remember the first time I had taco salad," said Mrs. Young to Lars. "Marybelle McCorkindale brought it to a luncheon..."

Abby finished lunch caught between two conversations, saying nothing. By the end of the meal she determined that Tammy would marry Duncan, and Lars would never again get stuck between two old ladies at breakfast.

"Patty?" Abby caught her as she whizzed past them. "Could you bring my check, please?" Patty stopped, reached into her apron and handed Abby the ticket.

"Mine too please," Duncan chimed in.

"Are you leaving already?" Lars had cleaned his plate and was still waiting for a break to get up for seconds.

"Yeah, my mom has to work this afternoon."

Duncan slid his chair out and held Abby's as she struggled with the legs on the carpet.

"Thank you." She could feel her face heat up and wished that she didn't blush at the drop of a hat.

"You bet."

"See you on Sunday." She waved at those still around the table.

"Bye." She heard Duncan behind her and soon felt his gentle hand on the small of her back again. She was warmed by the gesture. This time she did not move away.

Chapter 8

Duncan arrived in his office a full hour early so that he could pace the floor in peace. Angus had been in the kitchen finishing dinner when Duncan came in the night before.

"Who's the girl, eh? Duncan? Do we need to have Douggie write the prenuptial's already?" He grinned. "Kinda fast, isn't it, Duncan?"

"Nope." Duncan grinned and left the room before Angus could ask him anymore about the girl he didn't know what to do with. He had gone directly to his father's study. He couldn't very well tell Angus that he felt in his spirit that he needed to help this woman. She needed his protection and she was going to get it. But that didn't mean he was going to marry her, did it?

Once seated at the massive mahogany desk, he endeavored to work, but she interrupted him at every turn. He kept catching himself staring at nothing and wondering... Would she like the new boat? What was her favorite color? He would like to be there when she first slept aboard the sloop.

Thoughts of her sleeping near him got him up from his chair for a cup of coffee. He had been relieved to find Angus gone from the room.

Duncan managed to accomplish a few of the tasks he had assigned himself before retiring. It was late when he rose to go to bed. Thoughts of Abby ascended with him and remained until morning.

In the morning he paced the floor of his office. What was he going to do with her? His watch now said eight a.m. He'd been up and down this room for an hour. Time for coffee. Abby's interview wasn't until nine, so he'd be safe walking the hallways. While he didn't want to lie to her, he wanted her to be hired before she found out that he owned the place.

He consoled himself with the thought that he really hadn't had the opportunity to tell her anyway.

Chapter 9

Abby arrived at the MacLeod parking lot at 8:30 a.m., which was way too early for an interview at nine, but she was hoping she would be finished early so that she would have plenty of time to visit the Gordons before she had to pick up Chloe.

Mr. Oswald Gordon was a hospice patient whom Abby had met in her volunteer work at the hospital. Playing music for the terminally ill as a part of the hospice program at Ocean View General was one of the highlights of her week. She had become friends with both Mr. and Mrs. Gordon and looked forward to going to their house with her dulcimer. She dreaded the day when Mr. Gordon passed away.

Abby got out of the car to enjoy the view of the Bay. The wind was brisk and cold, a relief from the stuffy heat of the car. A gust lifted her hair up from her shoulders and kissed her neck. The gray-green water was tipped with white foam; the sky was quilted with steel blue clouds; the air smelled of a wood-fire.

MacLeod Tours was housed in a square, two-storied, stone fortress sitting on a thick sliver of land that pointed out to the Chesapeake Bay. Several boats were tied to finger docks that jutted from the bulkhead. Men were scurrying around attending to various tasks about which she hoped someday to understand more.

Abby walked up the brick steps to the front door. It was painted in black enamel, and felt more like a home than a business. She resisted the urge to knock and instead opened the door and stepped into a large room with wide slatted pine floors and white walls. She was welcomed by the source of the wood-fire smell she had enjoyed outside, a large stone fireplace. The room was immaculate and smelled of cinnamon. Abby introduced herself to a tall, blonde willow named Sandy who sat behind a large, highly polished, mahogany desk.

"Mr. Angus will be with you shortly."

"Thank you." The large room was sparsely furnished featuring only a large wooden desk for Sandy and a few wooden straight-backed chairs. Abby sat down in a straight-backed chair to wait. She had time to fully digest each pencil drawing of the boats on the Chesapeake Bay adorning the walls before the door opened and a giant man ducked through the door. He crossed the room in one step.

It was a miracle that he didn't shred his clothes in the doorway, she thought.

"Abigail Ericksen?" He reached to shake her hand.

"Yes." Abby stood and took his hand, which swallowed her own in a warm, brawny handshake.

"Angus MacLeod. I am pleased to meet you. Please follow me."

He turned and ducked back through the door. Abby followed him through to his office.

It was a small room that looked like it had once been a bedroom. It had one window that overlooked the Bay. On either side hung potted plants. A red oriental carpet covered the wide slatted pine floor. His desk was placed in front of the window. Two wooden straight-backed chairs like the ones in the front office were placed facing the desk and the window.

He held a chair for her to sit down, but when he sat down, Abby wished she could stand back up to look him in the eyes. His sandy, brown-red hair reminded her of the handsome stranger she had met at church. Mr. Angus MacLeod even wore a yellow plaid tie.

Yellow plaid must be in this year.

"Everything on your application seems to be in order." He folded his hands and rested them on top of an open file that she assumed must be hers.

"So tell me about yourself."

"I am a full-charge bookkeeper. I do payroll, taxes, accounts receivable and collectable."

"I see here that you organized the Old Thyme Festival last year."

"Yes."

"I went to that. How many people do you think you drew?"

It was the first time she had seen him smile. She relaxed a little.

"We sold 3,008 tickets, but that doesn't count the kids."

Angus regained his former composure.

"Why did you leave your previous employer?"

"He made requests that were beyond my ability to meet."

"That's interesting. May we contact him?"

"Yes." She hoped they wouldn't. She had no idea what kind of story Stanley would tell them.

"So what do you bring to us? Why do you think you would be an asset to our company?"

"I am honest, loyal and I work hard. I'll give you my best."

"You know we are not hiring a bookkeeper, but an assistant for her. You're overqualified for that."

"Yes, sir, but I need to work."

He looked down at the pile of paper on his desk as if he were deciding something. Abby looked out the window at the Bay. She folded her hands in her lap and tried not to shake. Couldn't he call her back and let her know?

"We're also hiring for another position."

Abby's eyes snapped back to his.

"We haven't advertised it yet, but with your experience, I think you can handle it. It's a cruise director. We are starting a new line of tours and we need someone to coordinate food and entertainments and the grand opening."

Abby could only listen. Would she get to go to sea?

"It would mean more money of course. Full benefits package—medical, dental, all the usual stuff. Would a full benefits package please you?"

Abby's mind swam. "I would like to look it over before I give you an answer."

"Certainly."

He continued to peruse the folder open before

him.

Abby couldn't believe it. What kind of an employer was this? She could not have scripted a better interview or written a better job offer.

"I understand you're a musician yourself. You'll be playing for our guests. Sing-along songs, stuff like that. We will train you of course in any other functions we may require. And provide a clothing allowance."

Abby was so excited that she had to will her body to be still. Her brain scrambled as usual when faced with the unexpected.

I'll take it. If it turns out wrong I can always quit. New clothes? Who did that nowadays?

"When can we expect to hear from you regarding our offer?"

"I accept."

Angus grinned. He stood up taking care not to bump the potted plant hanging from the ceiling.

"Glad to have you aboard. Now let's show you around. The big boss won't be ready for you for a while, so we have plenty of time for you to meet everybody."

Abby was walking on air. She was free. She could pay her bills and kiss Bradley good-bye. Everything was going to be OK. She was even going to have new clothes. Imagine. She couldn't wait to find Debbie and let her know she'd been hired. God had taken care of her again. Angus took her all over the building introducing her to everyone—first to Sandy, whom she had already met, and then to Andrew, his brother.

There was a strong family resemblance in the structure of their faces. They both had sandy-colored hair and brown eyes, but Andrew was much smaller than Angus. Angus had big steak hands; Andrew's were white and more delicate. While Angus carried himself seriously, Andrew had a fiendish twinkle in his eye.

Popular with the ladies, I expect. She'd seen that type before. Abby made a mental note to steer clear of him.

Grace was a sweet woman with a high-pitched voice who was in charge of reservations.

The bookkeeper's office, where Abby had planned to work, was adequate for the three desks it housed.

Debbie was not in. Her counterpart informed her that Rachel was sick. She sent up a silent prayer for healing and followed Angus to the canteen. It was empty but for the wooden tables and chairs and the hum of the coffee machine. Abby could almost hear the whisper of fish stories in the low drone of the room.

At noon, Angus led her to the office of the big boss and left her there. The reception area was small. His secretary was an older woman with salt-and-pepper hair and a purple ribbon tied in a bow on top. She smiled at Abby.

"He'll be with you in just a moment." She had the only Northern accent in the place. Her desk plate identified her as Lauretta.

"Have a seat." Lauretta went back to typing.

This time Abby had no thoughts of the pencil prints on the walls. She was filled with excitement about her new job. She sat with her hands clasped together on her lap and stared off into her dreams. She did not hear Lauretta right away.

"Miss Ericksen?" Lauretta repeated. Abby

looked up.

"He will see you now. Go right on in."

Odd for this place. Everywhere else she went, people had come out of their offices to meet her. Spoiled already, she laughed at herself as she walked past Lauretta into the office.

It was him—the man from the church. Her lungs deflated.

"Hello, Abby, I'm Duncan MacLeod." He was walking toward her with his arm stretched out for a handshake.

Abby stood there in silence. She didn't know what to do or feel. She didn't want to touch him; his electricity would only confuse her more.

"This is your family business?" She was embarrassed. She had told him of her dream of the sea. Had he been laughing at her?

No wonder. Angus—the resemblance was striking, another brother—was so happy to offer her a job she hadn't applied for. Oh yeah, this was funny all right. She had wondered if he had noticed her. He had noticed her all right and her need of new clothes. She felt tears well up behind her eyes. She took a deep breath and willed them away. Then she realized that he'd been talking. She couldn't see him or hear him. She could only feel shame.

Abby turned from him and walked out of the room. All the smiles she had encountered in this place were lies. Not that they knew ahead of time, but surely they would all have a chuckle when the joke was revealed. The cold air of the dock cut her skin and blew her hair off her shoulders, chilling her back.

"Abby." She heard his voice from behind her. "What's wrong?"

Abby could think of nothing to say. She wanted to leave. She blew on her hands and stood quietly in front of him.

"Don't you want to work with me? I promise not to ask you to go on a boat ride with a case of beer." He attempted a smile. Abby could not smile back.

"I was concerned that if you knew I owned MacLeod you wouldn't come.

Abby's face was frozen in humiliation. She had misread the whole thing.

He stepped forward and took her hands in his. His warmth radiated into her hands. She began to cry. He folded her into his arms.

"Everything was too good to be true." She cried into his shoulder. "When I saw you I thought it was a joke. I thought you were making fun of me."

It was Duncan's turn for silence. *Oh, God*, he prayed, *what has happened her?*

"I will never laugh at you, Abby." He looked down at her in his arms, and turned her face to him. It was wet with tears. His heart was pounding and breaking for her at the same time. He brushed his lips across her lips in the faintest of kisses before he realized what he was doing. He released her body and took a step back.

"Come with me." With a hand at her back he guided her around to face the dock and the cold wind coming off the water. Without touching, they walked to the empty side of the dock area.

"We have a new boat coming. We are going to do tours to Tangier. Overnighters. I want you to coordinate music and food. And then there's the grand opening. We will invite people from Richmond and even D.C. You're the person to coordinate all that."

The wind was chapping her wet face. She turned away from the dock to put the wind at her back.

"Why?"

"Because you're an excellent musician. I heard you play. And I like the idea of folk instruments— sort of a back-to-our-roots kind of thing. Sing-along songs around the cockpit..." He used his hands to illustrate.

"OK, look: I've only been on a boat once and I didn't do anything except sit around on the deck and get sunburned."

"I believe Angus told you that we will train you. Besides, you won't need to pilot the boat. You are to provide entertainments."

"How often will the boats be out? I have to think of Chloe."

"We will start them on Saturday's: Saturday morning to early Sunday afternoon. Just a little over twenty-four hours. As the season progresses they'll run every day of the week."

"I don't think I can do that. I have Chloe. My mom can do some babysitting, but I can't be gone all the time."

"I am sure we can work something out. By the time it becomes important we will have hired more people. You won't have to go every time. My brother plays guitar. At first we will be running only the one boat. Until I can hire another captain. My riverboats are not going to stop running. So I'll pilot the first one. As we get enough reservations we'll get another boat. When that one is reasonably full then we'll start a third."

"When do I start?"

"Tomorrow."

Chapter 10

Abby drove away from MacLeod Tours hopeful for her future. This could be the answer to her unspoken prayers. She could use her music. Could she have been wrong? Maybe her heart was on the right track this time. Perhaps she could relax and learn to trust again. She touched her lips, remembering his kiss.

On her way through the narrow neighborhood streets to visit the Gordons, she realized they must have some knowledge of Duncan MacLeod. Oswald Gordon worked for MacLeod for thirty years. He probably knew Duncan as a boy. She pulled into the Gordons' driveway.

Mr. Gordon had worked for MacLeod until his retirement two years ago. Abby had learned to play the first of her Celtic tunes to please him. He loved the pipes and her dulcimer, if tuned right, would give him the sound he relished. In his wife, Pat, she had found a mentor—a woman whose wisdom had come from a lifetime of walking with her Lord and living with a man she adored.

Pat greeted her at the door. Ossy was undergoing another round of chemotherapy and was too tired and weak to be doing anything more than resting.

"Is that Abby come to play with a sick old man?" The smiles in his voice gladdened her heart. Pat smiled and Abby returned the gesture. It was good to be here with these people.

The living room had been altered to accommodate a hospital bed and a couple of tables filled with medicines, bandages and other necessities of the terminally ill. Ossy lay on the bed, a thin replica of the robust man he used to be. Abby sat on a couch that had been pushed up against the wall to make room for the big bed. The room smelled of sickness.

"How are you, Ossy?"

He looked old today. His skin was white, his teeth, which used to fit his cheerful smile, were yellow and appeared too large for his skeletal face. A feeding tube from a small purse-sized bag rested beside the arm it was in. Abby's heart went out to him. Her problems were nothing next to those of this big man who was wasting away before her eyes.

"I'm doing as well as I expect to be. How's that baby of yours?"

His illness made him seem fierce.

"She's good. I'm picking her up early this afternoon to take her to the park or library or something."

"I hate to see kids in daycare." Ossy was nothing but direct as usual, but Abby was done feeling guilty about Chloe. She did the best she could and she knew that the Lord accepted that.

"Os," cautioned Pat, "don't say things like that

to Abby. She does the best she can with that baby. And she's such a sweet thing, too."

That Pat loved Chloe was evident in her gentle eyes. Ossy took the warning from his wife.

"How's work?" he asked, his voice still just as direct and fierce.

"Oh, well, I quit Stanley on Friday."

"Best thing you ever did, the bastard."

"Well, I start a new job tomorrow. I interviewed today with MacLeod."

Ossy got a faraway look in his eyes. Perhaps he was thinking of all those years on the water piloting riverboats.

"Lachlan MacLeod was a good man. I miss him. He used to come and see me. Like you do. I hear that his oldest son is in charge now. Stay away from him."

"Why?" Abby had figured that Ossy knew Duncan, but she had not expected this sort of a report.

"Os." Pat's gentle warning was soft and firm.

"Not this time, Pat. I watched that boy grow up. The best thing Lachlan ever did was send him away to the Army. Irresponsible and reckless, one girl after another. Just the kind of thing our Abby doesn't need."

By this time, he was sitting up and pointing his thumb at Abby.

"Listen to me, Abby. Stay away from him." He settled back down into the pillows at his back.

The pit of Abby's stomach began to twist. She was just beginning to think that maybe she was on the right track. Duncan had been so kind to her. Well, so much for that. At least she had a job, and that was nothing to sneeze at.

As if Pat could read her mind, she said, "Os, people can change. Especially if the Lord has anything to do with it. Duncan has been gone for ten years. You don't know him anymore."

Ossy didn't answer; he just closed his eyes.

"Mark my words, Pat, mark my words. Play me a jig on that thing today. Nothing sad."

He swiped the air a few times with his left hand. Abby shared a smile with Pat.

Abby began to play an old Scottish dance tune and followed it with two airs. As usual, he was asleep before she finished the third song. She let the last strum resonate away, parked her dulcimer in its case and followed Pat to the kitchen.

"You have a wonderful gift with that instrument. It reminds me of David playing for Saul and the evil spirit being driven away." Pat offered Abby a seat at the kitchen table. Abby sat while Pat put the kettle on.

"Thank you. You look tired. How are you holding up?"

"I'm doing as well as I expect to be."

They grinned at each other over her use of Ossy's words.

"How long have you known Duncan MacLeod?"

"I met him Saturday at family day."

"Oh, I wanted to be there. It seems quick for you to like him so well. Does he like you?"

Abby continually wondered at the insight of her friend.

"Well, there's no need to worry about that. I

have already decided that he's a no go."

"Why?"

"He's the second man I met at church. You know what happened the first time. Besides that I am going to work for him and I think you have to keep those things separate."

"Jesus changes people, Abby."

"Well, He hasn't helped Brad any."

"Brad has chosen not to be helped."

Chapter 11

Duncan crunched through the gravel parking lot to his truck and dumped off the work he was taking home. Zipping his coat, he walked out to the dock where his new fifty-foot boat was going to be moored. It was too cold to sit and let his feet dangle, so he leaned against the piling and stuffed his hands into his pockets. The smell of the Bay filled his nose. The wind was still up giving foamy caps to the wavelets. The water slapped against the dock. Ducks bobbed in and out of the pilings like bath toys.

Ever since the kiss in the parking lot Duncan could not get his mind off of Chloe. He was not sure if he was ready to be married, no matter that the kiss had intensified his attraction to Abby. If he wasn't ready to be married then he surely wasn't ready to be a father. The little girl with curly brown hair looked just like her mother, except for the blue eyes. Probably from her father, he reasoned.

If the man from the parking lot was her father, what had happened? Who could walk away from

Abby? She probably wasn't perfect, but he could see no serious flaws in her character. It was true he didn't know her all that well, but he was good at reading character, and he was willing to bet that in that situation Abby hadn't been the problem. How about Chloe? Didn't he know that children needed their fathers? And not just on the weekends either.

His own father was gone. There was nothing to replace the hours the two had spent planning out this next phase of their operations at MacLeod or the hours that his father had spent with him and his brothers teaching them about boats, about ropes, and wind, and clouds. The jokes they couldn't share with Mom.

It was a painful thing Lachlan had to do when he sent his son into the Army. Duncan was glad that he had. He needed to become a man and the Army with its discipline had done part of that for him. The accident had done the rest.

He could hear the laughter of the boys in the van. Some had been drinking; he had not. Lachlan had taught him to always be in control of his thoughts and actions and Duncan had experimented enough to know that he liked it better that way.

The van was careening alone down the four-lane highway at two in the morning. They were playing jump school. Jerry was the sergeant barking calls to the drunken men. All but Duncan. He was awake and ready for the risk. Mike was the first to jump out of the side of the van and roll across the empty right-hand lane and land in the grass on the other side. Next was Duncan. He steeled himself for the impact of the concrete by reminding himself that it's better to die as a good-looking corpse, and out he went. The air was warm;

the concrete was cold and hard. He rolled quickly to the grass. In the distance a spot of light caught the corner of his eye. He began to run to stop the van.

The car in the right-hand lane was weaving slightly to the right. Duncan moved closer to the trees on the right side of the grassy area where he had landed.

He could see John in the doorway of the van, hands braced on the roof, ready to fly out.

"No!" Duncan screamed.

John was laughing. He looked Duncan right in the eye and jumped.

If the man driving the white sedan had been sober he might have been able to get around John. Instead he smashed into the ball of a man and flattened him. If Duncan had not been so irresponsible they never would have done van jump school in the first place. Forgiveness had taken a long time. It finally came after long visits with John's widow, Connie, and becoming a member of her church. He accepted God's forgiveness and asked for forgiveness from Connie.

His life turned around. He contacted his father and they began to work on his life after he got out of the Army. His father had died before they had reached the first goal.

And now, here was Abby. He wanted to know her better. She was beautiful and smart, but she'd been hurt. If he was careful, held on loosely, and was patient, she might get better.

But Chloe. He wasn't sure he was ready to be a father.

His body was stiff from standing still in the wind for so long. The sun was beginning to set behind the clouds.

Chapter 12

"I'm not hundry," Chloe whined.

Abby stopped fixing the child's hot dog in time to see her throw up all over the table. After putting Chloe on the couch where she could watch her and scour the table, she dialed Brad.

The phone rang twice and then he picked up.

"Hello?"

No answer.

"Hello?"

Still no answer.

The phone didn't sound like it had been dropped.

One more time then she would hang up.

"Hello?"

"Hello, Abby?"

"Yeah, that was weird."

"What?"

"Our connection was odd like there was dead

space."

He said nothing.

"Anyway, Chloe just threw up all over the table so I can't bring her tonight."

"Oh. Is she OK?"

"Probably just a daycare stomach thing." *Which you would know about if you had ever taken care of your child.*

"She doesn't have a fever."

"Well, call me and tell me how everything went."

"Bye."

Chapter 13

"Don't answer the phone." Brad glared at Suzie who was sitting on the edge of the bed in the tiny yellow hotel room.

"What's the matter with you?" Suzie glared back at him and went back to blowing the paint job on her nails. "I'm expecting a call."

"You're the one who wants to keep everything a big secret, so don't answer the phone. Abby heard you answer." Brad felt more irritation than he could justify. He paced around the bed bumping into the television and the writing desk.

Ever since her miscarriage and finding out she couldn't have children, Suzie had been ranting on and on about going back to Ocean View. If she couldn't have a baby, then they'd get Chloe. When the transfer came through she'd been all over it like white on rice.

He didn't want to adopt. He didn't want any children at all. But if he had to have one he reckoned it should be his own flesh. So they'd come back to Ocean View. He hadn't planned on asking Abby to get back together. He just thought he'd check the place out and see how she and Chloe were getting along. Suzie said he should check to see if the house was dirty, but it wasn't. He had known it wouldn't be. Abby always kept a good, clean house. Unlike Suzie.

He didn't know what she did all day. She always seemed to be gone somewhere. She kept him happy elsewhere though, and that was the point. He didn't want a kid getting in the way of his lifestyle.

He didn't know what came over him that night with Abby. He just wanted her then and there. He hadn't even stopped to think what he would do with Suzie waiting back at the hotel for him.

"Who's gonna call you here?" he snapped.

"Julie. I met her when you and I first moved in together. You remember, don't you?"

Suzie perched on her knees on the edge of the bed. She grabbed his belt and pulled him to her.

"I just have to get out of here, honey. I've been packed away in this little room for days." She pouted.

"I still don't understand why we have to keep this all a big secret."

"Honey"—she began to unsnap his shirt—"you know that you are the man. That makes you the head of the household, so your daughter belongs with you. Especially now. Since I can't have anymore, which means you can't have anymore, we should have Chloe. Abby can have more children. Besides, what does she want with your kid anyway? I would never want my ex-husband's kid. Believe me, it's the best thing."

Brad removed her fingers from his hair and

snapped closed his shirt.

"Look, Suzie, this is serious stuff here. I've been over there. There is nothing to 'get' her with. The place is spotless. Chloe is clean. We should just leave our life as it is. Aren't I enough for you?"

"Of course you are, silly." She draped herself across the bed.

"It's just that I am so worried about Chloe. You know."

"No, I don't know. You never cared about Chloe until you miscarried. I'm sorry about that. And I've agreed to come this far, but I just don't know about the rest of this whole thing. I've checked on her, and she's fine. We should leave it at that."

"You should let the professionals look into it. You might not know what to look for."

"You don't know what you are getting us into. I hate to say this, but you've never had a baby, Suzie."

Her face fell. He lay next to her and folded her into his arms.

"I'm sorry, I'm so sorry. I never should have said that... I'm sorry... it's just that I like our life. No midnight feedings, no daycare. Just you and me. I like it that way."

"Oh Brad, please—just for me, look into it, please..."

"OK. OK."

Chapter 14

"Thanks for coming, Mom." Abby held the door open.

"Sure. No problem, hon." Helen brushed past Abby heading straight for the coffee pot. "You're right not to give it to the other kids at daycare. You give it to them and they wind up in the ER in the middle of the night."

"Chloe's still sleeping. I've got to get dressed."

Abby popped into the bedroom. She was grateful not to have time to sit down with Helen. She didn't want to tell her about Duncan. Not yet. Not until she knew what she was going to do with him.

Abby slipped into the blue jeans and a sweater she had laid out the night before. Then she combed her hair and began to braid it into one long plait down her back. There was no doubt that she was attracted to him. He was gorgeous, but it was more than looks that drew her. There was strength in him. Deep inside she sensed he was made of hard, unbending steel. It was the kind of strength she thought had died with her grandfather's generation, the kind that provides shelter in life's hurricanes. He was man, not boy.

Stop thinking like that. It's just a job. No complications.

She touched her fingers to her lips. That kiss had rocked her, but it probably hadn't affected him at all. Not if Ossy was right about his track record. The last thing Abby needed was another man to run around on her. She didn't want that for Chloe or herself. The next man, if there ever was one, would have to be picked by the Lord, and he would have to want both of them.

Was Pat right? Could Duncan have changed that much? Probably not. And strength without integrity and honesty could be very cruel. The real problem was figuring out how she was going to keep her distance from him while working next to him all day.

"Hello, honey." Helen's voice boomed through her door. Chloe was up.

Abby applied the final touches to her makeup and went to the kitchen. She wanted to have time to hold Chloe and prepare her for her day. The curly-headed doll was sitting on her grandmother's lap slowly waking up.

"I want Gramma," was all Chloe had to say to her mother's parting kiss.

The wind was blowing at the MacLeod dock. It was warm at sixty-five degrees and had all the earmarks of a day better spent outside. Abby scanned the parking lot for Duncan's truck. It wasn't there. She suppressed a pang of disappointment and smiled at Debbie as she got out of her car.

They fell in step together as they headed toward the building.

"How's Rachel?" Abby asked.

"Better. She had one of those throw-up flu things. I'm sorry I couldn't be here for you yesterday."

"Oh, it's OK."

"I hear it's better than OK. You got the job, huh?"

"Yes. I got a job. But it's not the one I applied for."

"Oh?" Debbie turned to glance at Abby but didn't slow her stride. "Gee. Gone for one day and I miss everything."

"You didn't tell me you worked for Duncan." Debbie looked puzzled. They stopped a few feet from the door.

"I do. Duncan MacLeod took over when his father died. There's some kind of family hierarchy thing. Angus has been here the longest, but Duncan inherits because he's the oldest."

"Have you met Duncan?"

"No. He's only been back here for a few days. Angus has been running things. I understand that he's been in touch with Duncan, though, through e-mails, that sort of thing."

"Duncan was the guy at church."

"No way."

"Way."

Debbie opened the door. Abby stepped through followed by her friend.

"Well, I'd better get going. Maybe I'll see you

for lunch. Do you know where you need to go?"

"Yes."

"Hi, Sandy!" Debbie called as she bopped off to her desk.

Abby walked down the hall to the open door of Angus's office. She was impressed this time more by the family resemblance than his size. The same sandy red hair and brown eyes, though his eyes lacked the warmth that she saw in Duncan's. The idea that she could bump into Duncan any minute thrummed through her body. What would she say to him?

"Come on in, Abby," Angus called to her over a mound of paperwork on his desk. Abby stepped into the office.

"Duncan's going to take you down to the dock to get you started."

She felt him there before she saw him.

"I thought it would help to give you an idea of what we do already for our day cruises. That way you'll get an idea of what we'll be looking for in the new boat," Duncan said placing a hand on her elbow and gently leading her through the door.

"Sounds good." She tried to sound confident despite the electric, spiking nerves that were checking in up and down her back. Fresh air on her face drew her attention from her emotions; just being outside was a blessing. The braid down her back kept the friendly breeze from lifting it off her neck. Three white ferryboats bobbed at the dock. Duncan took large strides to get to them. Abby nearly ran to keep up.

"The boats seem high. Is it high tide?"

"Just past. The time of the tide changes every

day. If it's high tide today at say, eight, then tomorrow high tide will be at eight-forty. It cycles."

"So that's why we hear it on the radio all the time."

"Yep. Now, we don't have the ramps up yet. They're being painted for the new season, so you'll just have to hop across."

Duncan nimbly stepped up from dock to boat. He turned and offered his hand to Abby.

Abby stepped gingerly across and crammed herself next to Duncan on the narrow walkway that led around the entire deck. They were standing in front of a row of box-benches. It was a viewing deck, she surmised. She couldn't imagine how it would feel with ten people on board—let alone the fifty it was supposed to handle.

"How much do you know about boats?" Duncan asked.

"They float."

"That much?"

"I told you that the other day."

"Well, we'd better start at the beginning. This is the stern, or back of the boat. The front is the bow."

"OK."

"Left side is port." He pointed left in case she wasn't sure of her directions.

"Right side is starboard." He pointed right. He showed her everything: things that she was sure she wouldn't need, like where the anchor was kept, to things that she might need to know, like where the life preservers were kept, to the most important thing to her—the storage bins. The whole boat was ringed with them. They were found under the box seats with an even larger one behind the bar counter in the cabin.

"Of course a sailboat isn't this big," Duncan said. They were standing on the bow.

"No, I guess it couldn't be, could it," Abby responded and looked directly into his eyes. They were soft brown in the sunlight. She looked quickly out toward the water.

"Abby, I owe you an apology. I never should have kissed you the other day. It was out of line, and I..." Abby felt her face flame and her thoughts scatter.

"It's OK." She took a step away from him, knelt down in front of a box bin, and stuck her head in one of the compartments.

"The one's on the new boat, will they be this big?"

"Abby." He gently pulled her to her feet. "Look, I like you, but I think if we are ever going to mean anything to each other, we have to go slow. There are things about me you don't know, and I barely know you."

"Isn't that the truth."

"I want to know you better, just slowly." He brushed a wisp of hair from her eyes. Abby felt his current pulling her to him. She stepped away.

"Are we done here?" Her voice sounded too abrupt to her ears.

"How'd he do last night?" A gravelly voice came from behind them as they stood by the railing.

"First place."

"I knew he'd do it."

Like ripples in a smooth pond, the man's face wrinkled in waves to a near toothless grin. He wore a dark blue work jumper dotted with white paint.

His wispy, white hair danced in the breeze.

"I'll tell him you said so, Jack." Then Duncan turned to Abby. "My brother races sailboats."

"Who's the pretty girl?" Abby smiled and offered her hand to the old man.

"This is Abby. She's going to organize our new cruises."

"That's a big job, Missy. Can ya do it?"

"Yes, sir." Abby smiled at Jack.

"Abby organized the Old Thyme Festival last year, Jack."

"I was there. Ya need more sea songs at that thing. It was good, though."

"Do you know any?"

"Course I do." He patted the harmonica in his front pocket. "Well, I gotta get back. I can't stand round here all day."

"I'd like to hear you play sometime." Abby tossed out as he walked away. He nodded over his shoulder and shuffled away.

Duncan showed her around the rest of the ferry without any further fanfare. She took in what she could, knowing she could return if necessary. She spent the rest of the afternoon getting acquainted with the rest of the place.

Abby pulled onto the concrete pad that served as her driveway amid the squeals of Chloe.

"Momma! Momma!" Chloe yelled as she ran the short distance to the car.

Abby nearly rolled out onto the ground in her speed to get out of the car to grab her little girl on bended knee.

"Hello, punkin'." The little body next to her

heart was joy. Stress melted into laughter.

"Let's go out," Helen announced, emerging from the back door.

"She seems to be better. Is she up to it?"

"Absolutely. She had a little bit of lunch. But she's been asking for supper since three."

"I don't know, Mom. I don't want to run into Brad."

"Why would we?"

"I don't know—I just have a feeling, you know?"

"Don't be silly. We'll be fine." She dropped her hand from her wrist. "It'll be good to get out for a while. I'll run in and get my purse."

"Yeah," Abby said, but she wasn't sure. She really felt like she should stay home and have a can of soup. After all, she'd been out all day. But Mom's the expert, she reasoned. If she says Chloe's OK then it's probably all right. If that nagging doubt would just go away, then she'd feel better about it.

Chloe pulled at her back pocket. Blue eyes, big smile.

"Let's go Sammy's!"

"OK, punkin'." Helen came out with a small diaper bag and her purse. They all piled into Helen's car.

"I don't know why this feeling won't go away. He didn't even like Sammy's. He thought the whole buffet thing was gross. I used to go to a Sammy's with my good friend Suzie."

The two laughed and Helen drove them to Sammy's.

It was early for dinner when they arrived at the

restaurant. Before they walked in, they could see Sharmagne standing behind the counter.

"Hey, y'all." Sharmagne's face broke into a big wide grin.

"Hey, Sharmagne."

"Y'all want to sit by the windows?" She grabbed a couple of menus.

"We missed you on Sunday. Is everything OK?" Abby asked.

"Yeah. I was working my other job. But you know, the good Lord, He knows that I gotta do what I gotta do to take care of my babies."

"Yeah, He does."

"You let me know if you need anything, hear?"

"Sure will."

Abby faced the view of the parking lot, Helen faced the inside of the room and Chloe sat in a high chair at the end between them. Abby and Helen took turns at the salad bar. Chloe was happy with cubes of ham and cheese and wedges of tomato. When they were settled back at the table with plates full Helen dove in.

"So how was it?"

"It's only been one day. I didn't do much." *Except my boss is made of electricity.*

She smiled at her mother. "It's gonna be like a bed and breakfast on the water. I have to plan menus and all that kind of stuff. Have you ever been to Tangier Island?"

"Isn't that where they still talk like the old English settlers?"

"I think so."

"I have heard about it, but I've never been

there. Is that where you'll be going?"

"Yep."

Brad's green truck pulled into the parking lot and took the space across from where Abby was sitting. She held her fork suspended as she glanced from Brad to Suzie. Betrayal is a cold zephyr: it blows through the body from the nape of the neck outward. Her spine shivered in its wake. Brad turned away from her to get out of the truck.

She left him, did she?

Before Abby could collect her thoughts, he was standing at her side, holding hands with Suzie.

"I thought she was sick." He smirked.

"She was. My mom stayed with her today. She's better now."

"Good. I'll be able to see her in the next couple of days then."

"Hi, Suz'. Nice to see you," Helen pitched in. Abby had to lean forward to see Suzie still holding hands and hiding behind Brad. Suzie raised an eyebrow in response.

"Would you all like to sit together?" Sharmagne addressed Brad.

"Ah, no. That's OK."

"Well, if you would follow me, I'll show you to your table."

"I'll call you," he said, and they left. Sharmagne sat them in a booth close to the entrance. Abby would have to walk by the two of them when they left. Great.

"I knew we shouldn't have come," Abby said when he was out of earshot. "I don't think I can eat now."

"How could we know that we'd run into him here? Even you said he doesn't like the place." Helen picked up her fork and continued with her meal.

"I know, Mom. It's not your fault." *I should have just listened*, she said to herself, not for the first time.

Abby pushed her plate away. Chloe pushed her plate away, too. She seemed to be done. Abby pulled out a baby wipe and cleaned her fingers and face. By the time she was done cleaning Chloe, Helen was ready to go. Helen picked up the check and they headed down the gauntlet. Brad was facing them as they walked toward the checkout near the entrance.

"Hi, Da—" Chunks flew before she could finish. Little pieces of ham dressed in pungent, frothy, yellow gunk landed on Brad's pants, and all over the floor. Chloe started to cry.

"My pants!" He took a paper napkin and swiped at the mess.

"Gross!" Suzie said.

Sharmagne appeared at Abby's elbow and said, "It's all right, honey. You just take care of that baby. I'll take care of this mess."

Abby picked up the crying Chloe, and carried her to the bathroom. She sat her child on the edge of the sink and cleaned her up. After Chloe calmed down, they left without another glance at Brad and Suzie.

"I think you had better call Social Services and get them to intervene. She obviously isn't taking care of Chloe. What kind of a mother takes a sick kid out to a restaurant to eat?"

"You're right."

Chapter 15

The next two days ticked by a notch at a time.
Abby contained her anger by rattling around in
her apartment. She cleaned until her hands were
red. What had Brad meant by asking her to
reconcile? Tears of frustration burned her eyes
when she wasn't banging her knuckles on some
fixture she was scrubbing. Suzie had been in the
background the whole time. *Had she known?*
Maybe. *Why did Brad think he could use me that
way?*

What if I had said yes?

And Duncan? She wasn't ready. She couldn't
trust anyone. Not yet. Maybe not ever.

By Friday, Chloe was better, and Abby returned
to work. She found that she had been given the only
empty desk to be found. It was in Debbie's office.
Later that morning, Angus dropped off a stack full
of catalogues and a book on boating safety from the
Coast Guard. She spent the rest of the day going
through catalogues and becoming more acquainted
with her friend Debbie and her office mate, Kay.

Debbie and Abby had been church friends. Because of their small children, neither of them had the time to devote to friendships other than the casual kind that develop in groups where people see each other repeatedly in settings where little talk is possible. Lunchtime became a time of fellowship.

Abby put down the last catalogue in time for lunch. The women preferred to eat outside on the picnic table that was provided for that purpose. Abby sat across from Debbie and Kay. Kay was a small, blonde woman with pearly white teeth and a loose tongue.

"I think I know why we have not heard or seen Mr. Duncan MacLeod since Tuesday," Kay declared while pinching a dainty morsel off the corner of her sandwich and placing it on her tongue. "I think he's hiding from us."

Abby couldn't imagine Duncan MacLeod hiding from anyone. But then she didn't know him very well. They had only shared a kiss after all. As he had been quick to point out, that didn't mean you knew a person.

"Why?" Abby asked. Debbie rolled her eyes—a gesture Abby was sure Debbie would have kept to herself if Kay could have seen it.

"Because it's a disgrace that he is taking over this company from his brother. It rightfully belongs to Mr. Angus. It's just not fair that it was given to Duncan. He's ashamed to show his face, " she said and took a sip of her diet soda.

"Why would he care what we think? It doesn't make sense."

"We're like family to them. That's why." Debbie agreed with this by nodding her head.

"What do you mean—like family?"

"That part is true." Debbie took over. "The MacLeod's treat all their employees like family. When you were hired, didn't you think that they made you a generous offer?"

Abby had not thought until this moment that Debbie would know about her financial arrangements. But of course she would. As the bookkeeper, Debbie would write her checks.

"Yes, I did."

"They treat everyone like that. They are generous with holidays, too. Of course it's handy that the important ones fall in the winter when we are nearly shut down anyway. But I don't think that Mr. Duncan is trying to stay away from us because he's afraid to show his face. I think he must have some kind of work to keep him busy outside of the office."

Debbie's arguments sounded much more grounded than Kay's accusations.

"Whatever you say, I still think that there'll be a falling out over this. Duncan had no right to come here and take over what Mr. Angus had earned by rights."

They finished their lunch and went back to work. Abby had no time to reflect on Kay's comments until she drove home.

Maneuvering her car through the narrow streets toward home, Abby dismissed the idea that her presence had kept him from coming to work. He was right after all: there was a lot she didn't know about him, and what she had heard wasn't promising. She felt now that some time had passed she would be able to deal with him in a friendly fashion without a hint of romance. After all, they had to work together, and she knew how to be professional—despite running out of the room during the interview. She had never done that kind of thing before. She still felt red faced every time it crossed her mind.

As for a falling out with Angus, she hoped it wouldn't come to that. But even if it did, it wouldn't be her business. Abby patted the pocket of her jeans where her first paycheck lay folded. She said a prayer to thank God for the money and Duncan MacLeod for giving her the job. Maybe she would see him again on Sunday.

Chapter 16

Duncan spent Saturday driving home from Fort Bragg, North Carolina. It had taken three days to muster out of the Army. He was relieved it was over. He was now on his journey home. He thought of the quiet passing of the citizen soldier. How many had gone home just this way? He was driving, but many of them would have walked down dusty roads. How many of them had come home to no fanfare whatsoever? No ceremony to mark their passing. Just forms and paperwork and, "*You're good to go, Soldier.*"

He had never seen combat, yet he was proud of his career. Except for the accident, his career had been successful. He had stood watch in peacetime. He was satisfied. True, he did not have the farewell of generals. It was enough that he had done his duty and done it well.

Now he was free to concentrate on the business at hand. Thoughts of home turned to his mother and father. Lachlan MacLeod had recorded his courtship of the beautiful Erin Dalrymple in the

Chronicles.

Lachlan's mother, Maureen O'Toole MacLeod, held a big party at Easter every year. She called it "Easter on the Lawn" and invited everyone she knew. It was she who persuaded Lachlan to invite the young Erin Dalrymple. Erin, the beatnik, had to be cajoled into coming. Full of stories about Jack Kerouac and the road, she would have nothing to do with convention.

Maureen O'Toole MacLeod was a forthright woman, warm and affectionate. It didn't take her long to recognize her Lachlan's attachment to Erin. So she created an opportunity to tell the odd story of how she came to be a MacLeod.

A big grin spread across Duncan's face. Mother was a beatnik. He snapped his fingers and laughed. He could just see her on bended knee in front of Lachlan. Back straight, she still wouldn't have come up much past his knee.

"You would make me the happiest woman in the world," she had said to Lachlan, offering the ring, which he wore to the grave.

Perhaps they needed to have another "Easter on the Lawn" this year, he thought fiendishly.

Perhaps he would see Abby on Sunday.

Chapter 17

The parish house of Bethel of the Bible Church was built of cinder block. Inside it was painted with white enamel like an elementary school. In the basement were several rooms and a kitchen. Abby's Sunday school class met in a corner room. Small rectangular windows studded the walls near the ceiling.

It was a foggy, wet morning. Dampness had seeped into the room making it an ice box. Abby was glad she had her cardigan. Huddled around the large rectangular table were Mrs. Young, Mrs. Petersen, Mrs. Bennett, and Duncan. Abby was relieved to see Tammy was absent. Abby took an open seat across from Duncan.

Lars sat at the head of the table and read out the usual list of announcements in a breathy, baritone with theatrical pauses between each.

"Our Sunday school class is having a picnic next Sunday afternoon at my house for anyone who wishes to come." Lengthy pause for writing down essential points.

"Anyone who can make it is welcome to help with a yard sale for the youth on Saturday morning at seven." Another lengthy pause. Then he prayed, and after a pause, he read from Matthew 18.

"Seventy times seven," he breathed. "We are to forgive our brother seventy times seven." He paused and looked around the table. "You know, I've been thinking about that, and it doesn't seem that hard to me to forgive people." He looked down, paused once more, and continued, "Perhaps it's what Christ has done for me. I don't know." He swiped his left hand, palm up in a gesture that said it was beyond him to fathom the reason. "Does anyone have anything to say about that?"

This part was always awkward. Everyone waited to see who would be first. None of them wanted to appear over eager. Pairs of eyes scanned the others at the table and then looked down at whatever lay before them on the table, waiting to see who would take the plunge. Mrs. Young's large blue eyes were distant and rimmed in pink as if she'd had a cold or had been crying recently. Mrs. Bennett looked out at the table blankly. Mrs. Petersen kept her eyes down at her Bible reading ahead and behind the passage they were studying. Duncan sat across from Abby with his Bible open.

Abby didn't mind starting usually, but this time guilt had short-circuited her brain. She condemned herself a hypocrite. Why did they have to talk about forgiveness of all things? Duncan piped in before Abby could come up with a valid point.

"I think that it's always hard to forgive someone who's hurt you. But I do believe that before healing can take place, forgiveness must happen."

Did Duncan mean to talk to her? Nah, he didn't

even know about Brad.

"Yes, I would agree with that," breathed Lars. "We are all so imperfect; we all need forgiveness."

"I am having a hard time with this one," said Mrs. Young. There was an edge to her usually mild voice. "Last week my daughter left her husband and moved in with me. She will not talk about it with me. She won't talk to him." Mrs. Young paused, looked around at all of them, and continued, her eyes filling with tears.

"On top of it all, my social security check went missing." She choked and her eyes brimmed over, the tears landing on tissue as she dabbed her eyes. "I'm afraid she took it." She paused to strengthen her voice. "I don't know what to do. I've never been in a situation like this." She looked back down at the table and dabbed her eyes once more, trying to calm herself.

Again they waited, like people at a gravesite, not knowing what to say or how to say anything.

Mrs. Young continued to look down.

Abby looked from face to face.

"Maybe it's drugs." Mrs. Young choked on the words.

"Vengeance is mine, I will repay, says the Lord," Mrs. Bennett offered.

"That is so true. You know, I just read the oddest thing on the Internet." Mrs. Petersen looked up with her eyes open wide. "Voltaire went about the world telling people that the Bible was outdated and that by the end of his generation, no one would be reading it anymore. Of course not only were they still reading it, but a hundred years later, his own printing press was used to print Bibles." They all smiled awkwardly at the story.

"Have you called the police?" Duncan asked Mrs. Young.

"No, I tried to mention it to Ruth, but she didn't seem to know anything. But she didn't really answer; she doesn't want to talk to me. She's so sullen, and I hate to say it but ... *rude*." She stopped to adjust her tissue and dab her eyes again. "She's usually so sociable." Again she struggled for control. "I did call the Social Security people. They said that they have to wait to see if the check clears. And if it does, then they will compare the signatures. If they can tell it's not mine, then they will reissue a check. If it doesn't clear, then they will reissue a new check."

Abby was overcome with frustration. How long was an old person supposed to wait for her only income to arrive? Didn't those people realize that it was all she had to live on?

"How about changing your address—get a P.O. box?" Duncan said, thoughtfully rubbing his hand over his mouth and chin.

"Yeah, that'll keep her away from it," said Mrs. Bennett.

Mrs. Young's problem seemed very black and white to Abby. Tell the daughter to get out. Get her some help maybe, but not at home. But who was she to tell the older saint what to do? She still couldn't figure out what to do with Brad. Abby was tired of trying to forgive Brad and tired of feeling guilty for not forgiving him.

"Isn't Christianity supposed to have some teeth?" Abby shot out onto the table. "Doesn't it say that when a brother continues to walk disorderly that we are to evict him from the assembly? Look at Jesus and the money changers in the temple. I think he must have been huge."

Heads bobbed up and down in agreement. The pages in Mrs. Petersen's Bible sounded like rain on the windowsill as she flipped around trying to find the passage Abby referred to.

"It does say that," answered Duncan, "but you are not allowed to have resentment towards that person."

"Well, I'm not talking about that. If someone, like Mrs. Young's daughter, hurts you and threatens you with harm, I think that even as Christians we have a right to stand up for ourselves."

Mrs. Young looked up.

"Of course, Jesus never said we had to be door mats." Duncan smiled at her.

Abby's heart yanked itself into overdrive.

"I don't think money changers have anything to do with it. I think you have to be very careful about this. Don't forget the other cheek," Lars threw in.

"We aren't talking about 'other cheek' kind of situations," Duncan countered.

The loud ringing of the Sunday school bell brought to a close the discussion. They ended with prayer and they filed out to meld into the larger group pooling in the kitchen and trickling out the various exits. Abby watched Duncan catch up with Mrs. Young as she walked past the kitchen on her way toward the hallway to Chloe's classroom.

"Momma! Momma!" Chloe shouted and ran to Abby's waist.

"Hello, punkin'. You ready?"

Abby gathered Chloe's papers and thanked Debbie. Duncan was leaning against the wall when she came out. Their eyes met. He followed her outside into the bright March day.

She blinked rapidly in the brilliant sunlight. The dampness of the morning had burned off, but the ground was still soggy. Abby kept her heels carefully on the pavement.

"Would you like to go to Sammy's?" Duncan asked.

The last place in the world she wanted to eat was Sammy's.

"No, thanks. Chloe and I are going home to eat." He looked disappointed. Her heart warmed toward him. She couldn't help but smile. "What do you think of grilled cheese?" she asked.

"It's been a long time since I had one." He smiled back and her heart skipped a beat. Dangerously handsome was right.

"You're welcome to eat with us if you like."

"All right. I'll follow you," he replied

Abby was not usually embarrassed of her home, but today was different. As she turned onto Parkview Avenue, she felt like she should have agreed to go anywhere with him but home. He had to be used to much better. Her apartment with its orange carpet was a tenement compared to the mansion he probably lived in.

At least it's clean.

"Can't help what you can afford. Can help how clean it is." Her grandmother's words whispered in her memory. She hadn't thought about that in years.

To make matters worse, when she pulled into the driveway Helen's car was sitting there. Her mom had a key to her apartment and must be waiting inside. Abby parked the car, took a deep breath, and got out. Chloe hopped out and ran to the duplex yelling,

"Gramma! Gramma!"

The call brought a smile to Abby's face. She turned that smile up to Duncan who smiled back.

"She does that a lot," he said.

"Yeah, she does. It's a joy. Do you have any children?"

Duncan's eyes widened.

"I have never been married," he replied.

"Well, that doesn't seem to mean much anymore." She cast her eyes down to walk through the spongy ground.

"True," he said as they headed across the grass toward the apartment.

"Listen, before we go in... My mom is here. I didn't know she would be here."

"It's OK. I would like to meet your mom."

That's nice, Abby thought, *but I don't want her to meet you.* Her mother didn't even know about him.

Chapter 18

To Duncan the dim room was like stepping into a closet to find a lost shoe.

Details came into focus slowly as his eyes adjusted. It was sparsely decorated. One round table with four chairs in what could only be described as a kitchen/dining room combo, a bamboo and wicker love seat, and one chair in the living room. There was a small television with a video machine. The windows were ordinary except for the white metal bars that encased them. Despite their plainness the rooms were warm and inviting. He felt at home and comfortable at once.

"Please have a seat." Abby directed him to a chair on the far side of the round table that dominated the kitchen/dining room combo.

"My mom is helping Chloe change. They'll be out in a minute." Abby offered him iced tea, which he accepted.

When she turned her back to him to prepare salad. He stood up and went to stand next to her.

He picked up a carrot slice and munched.

"So how long have you lived here?"

"About a year now." Abby blushed that attractive pink. Her back stiffened.

"It's nice."

"It's not. But it's what I can afford, and I keep it clean." She kept her face to her work.

"Well, I like it."

"Surely you are used to much better." She cast him a sideways glance.

"In the Army? You gotta be kiddin'. Our barracks at Ft. McCall were covered in tar paper."

"Now you're kidding." She pointed a carrot at him and gave him a direct look that he interpreted to mean "you better tell me the truth or else." But she began to relax; the lines of her body became fluid once more.

Then, a short, trim woman wearing purple hospital scrubs came out of the back of the apartment holding Chloe's hand. Her hair was short and brown like her granddaughter's. She wore silver rings on three fingers of each of her hands. Her eyes were challenging. He could tell she was not the type of person who gave anyone the benefit of the doubt.

"Hi, I'm Duncan MacLeod." He extended his hand. The woman stepped forward to clasp his hand. Chloe broke free and returned to the back of the house. He assumed she'd gone back to her bedroom.

"Helen Roberts." She shook hands like a man.

"I met Duncan at church, Mom. He's gonna have lunch with us."

Helen smiled at him. Coffee had stained her

teeth. Helen poured herself a cup and sat down at the table.

"Whatcha makin'?" she hollered to Abby.

"Grilled cheese and salad."

"Do you work at the hospital?" Duncan asked as he sat down across from her. He was prepared for the challenge in Helen's eyes.

"Yes. What do you do?"

"I own a family business. As a matter of fact, Abby has just started to work for me. MacLeod Tours."

"So you're that Duncan MacLeod."

"Yes, ma'am."

"I knew your father." Recognition glowed from Helen's eyes.

"How did you know him?" Duncan wished with all his heart that the pain he felt when anyone mentioned Lachlan would ease.

"I was with him that last night in the ER. I am so sorry he's gone. How's your mom doing? She was pretty bad that night." Concern mellowed the fierceness he had encountered on her entry. "She was so calm. I thought the quietness would break her back."

"She's doing all right. They were very close."

"I could see that. She stayed with him all night that night. I don't think I saw her sit down even once."

Abby served up the sandwiches. Duncan waited for grace. Helen took a bite of her sandwich. Duncan looked to Abby. She was holding hands with Chloe. They closed their eyes together in silent prayer.

"So, Abby tells me you're buying a new boat to go to Tangier," said Helen as if she hadn't noticed the prayer.

Duncan spent the rest of lunch telling them about the boat he had chosen and why. Chloe watched him with big eyes through the entire meal. He was reluctant to leave, but after the meal was over, he could think of nothing more to discuss with Helen and Abby. If Abby had been on her own, he imagined they could have gone for a walk and talked about nothing much for hours.

After walking him to his car, Abby went back to the house with a warm glow deep down. Why had she been so concerned about Helen? Helen worked with people who were in need all the time. And she was good at her job. Abby knew people all over Ocean View who loved her mom. Everything had gone so well.

It hadn't occurred to her that Helen could have been there the night Lachlan MacLeod died. She wondered what kind of man he was. Maybe this one was going to turn out OK. He hadn't looked down on her apartment; he even said he liked it. That could be nothing but kindness. The screen door slapped shut behind her as she went back inside.

"Be careful of that one." Fierceness was back with a vengeance in Helen's voice and eyes.

"Why? He seems nice enough."

"I was in the ER one night with him, too."

"What happened? Was he hurt?"

"I can't remember the details. Let me think about it. Just trust me on this one. Give him some distance."

"Gosh, Mom, it's not like we're getting married tomorrow or anything."

"Just listen to me. That one's trouble." Helen banged her hand, palm down, on the table for emphasis.

"OK, OK," Abby agreed. She turned from Helen to the sink to clean up the dishes and hide the hot tears at the corners of her eyes. This was the honesty she had asked for; she didn't want any more mistakes. But Duncan had felt right to her in a way that Brad never had. And though she hadn't invested anything in their relationship, she knew her heart was definitely looking his way.

Chapter 19

"Everybody thinks that Angus should have gotten the place. You should see him sail. He wins every time at the Monday night boat races." Monday lunch at the picnic table. It was glorious outside. The sun was shining in the blue sky and the breeze was steady. Kay's rhetoric had not changed. Duncan shouldn't have inherited the business and on and on in praise of Angus MacLeod.

"What're Monday night boat races?" Abby hoped to change the subject.

"They're put on by the local yacht club, and Angus MacLeod always wins. I've heard some say that he should have tried for the America's Cup."

"A guy from this little burg?" Debbie was incredulous.

"He's won all the local stuff. The lighthouse race, the Monday night races—he's even won the bathtub race put on by the university."

Duncan arrived out of nowhere carrying a

paper bag and a sweating bottle of water.

"Hi. Do you mind if I join you?" He smiled into Abby's eyes. Her pulse quickened. She smiled back.

"Of course not. You sit here." Debbie shot Abby a conspiratorial look. She got up quickly and moved to Abby's side of the table. Abby slid over to make room. Kay stayed put, straightening her back just a little, and turned ever so slightly toward him. He sat down and pulled out a deli-sized sandwich on rye and a baggie of fig bars. He was still for a flash and then picked up the sandwich and took a bite.

"So how do you find Ocean View on your return?" Kay's mistimed question resulted in a bobbing of his head and a hurried chew and swallow.

"I like it." His response was directed at Abby.

"Look at the time." Debbie pointed to her watch, and looking at Kay said, "Time to get back in."

Abby gathered her wrappings, disappointed at the need to pull away from Duncan. She wanted to stay and learn more about him.

"Abby, stay. I need to talk to you." Duncan supplied the excuse she needed.

Her companions left for the office, and she sat back down. "What about?"

Duncan looked past her. She glanced behind her to see her coworkers opening the door and stepping inside.

"Mrs. Young." He took another bite of the sandwich.

Abby watched him. His shirt stretched over work-made muscles. His arms ended in thick-fingered hands. His lips glistened as he took a drink of cold water. A tingly warmth spread through her as she remembered the feel of his lips on hers. She shifted on the bench seat and looked up into his eyes, which had caught her staring. She felt her face redden; he smiled.

"I thought we should go and see her. I would like to help her out, but it's a little awkward."

"Why? You're a member of the church. She's a widow."

"She *is* a widow, but I am a stranger to her."

You're not much more than that to me either, she thought to herself. At the same time, she felt she knew him better. That same inexplicable feeling of trust was still there.

"Sure, I'll go with you."

"Great, we'll go after lunch."

"Are you sure? I'm supposed to be working."

"Yes, I'm sure. There's nothing much for you to do yet. Angus told me he gave you every catalogue he could find and the book from the Coast Guard."

"He did."

"Well, you must be done with that by now. And the Coast Guard book all by itself isn't enough. You'll have to take the class." He ate the last bite of his sandwich.

Abby was relieved to hear it. She couldn't make up anything else to do, and Angus had no more assignments to give her. She had asked him that morning. So if Duncan was going to pay her to do God's work, then so be it.

Besides, she had been worried about Mrs. Young, but she wasn't sure how she could help since she had no experience with drug addicts. Perhaps together they could at least find out if help was needed.

Abby was sitting within kissing distance of Duncan MacLeod in the small pickup truck. She could feel the warmth of his body radiating out to her, enticing her to reach out and touch him. But she knew from their past encounters that her touch would not be welcome. He wanted to get to know her, he had said, and intellectually, she had to agree that going slowly was wise, but that didn't seem to slow the growth of her desire for him. She needed to think about something else.

Why was he so interested in Mrs. Young? Did he know her daughter? Was she the reason that Duncan was in the emergency room ten years ago? Her thoughts drifted wildly from one thing to another. Perhaps it was a car accident? Perhaps an abortion went wrong? Dim light began to dawn in her brain. Perhaps he knew all about drug addicts. Was he a junkie gone straight?

Her instincts told her that he was OK and that nothing so sinister lay hidden in his past, but her instincts were never right. She shouldn't even be here. She had promised her mother.

"This looks like the place." Duncan parked in the driveway.

Mrs. Young came to the door wearing a blue housecoat painted in large orange flowers. She smelled of baby powder. Abby was surprised to see her dressed in an outfit she had only seen on very large women.

"Hello, Abby, Duncan—isn't it? Please come in."

They stepped in onto a clear plastic runner in a yellow-beige room. It was a small, meticulously clean room. A faint smell of mint lingered in the humid air.

Mrs. Young led them on the runner to the dining room table.

"Would you care for tea?"

Abby and Duncan looked at each other. Their stomachs were full, but both accepted her offer.

"We'll need to be quiet. Ruth is sleeping."

Abby forced her face not to react. Still sleeping at this hour? Duncan took an offered seat at the table. Behind the table were two windows overlooking the back yard. A huge vegetable garden was laid out: rows of turned up soil; new brown stakes with white tags fluttering on their tops; and little green shoots just peeking out of stems of fruit trees.

"You've been working a good bit." Duncan pointed to the windows.

"Yes." She smiled at the garden through the windows. "I got started gardening during the war, with my folks. A victory garden, you know. I just never stopped. There is nothing like a fresh cuke in the summer. Just wouldn't be summer without the fresh cukes."

She turned to face them, her blue eyes full of sunlight.

"Mr. Young used to make the best pickles you ever ate. I make them now, but I don't have his touch." She wrung her hands. She stepped into the kitchen to get the iced tea. She served them in golden glass tumblers. Duncan and Abby eyed each other. What were they going to do now? Abby, for some reason, had thought that they were going to walk in on a mess: a house mess, a life mess. Except for the sleeping woman, this was all very tidy.

"So why did you want to see me?" Mrs. Young asked after they were settled.

"We were worried about you. Are you all right?"

"I am. I'm OK. I am still worried about my daughter."

"That's why we came."

"Let's go out back."

Chapter 20

Abby and Duncan followed Mrs. Young out the kitchen door and into the backyard. The windows had given an illusion of a minor estate. The reality was less than a third of an acre surrounded by a chain-link fence. She led them to a set of plastic hunter green stackable deck chairs. The yard was dry; the foliage had not yet opened to give it the misty cool of a flourishing garden.

"Like I said before, I'm worried about my daughter. Homer and I raised her in the church, we did all the right things..." Her voice trailed off.

Abby had met Ruth Young, now Abercrombie, twice a year on the holidays when Ruth and her dashing husband came to church with her mother. She was a regal beauty, cast in porcelain: creamy skin, dark curly hair, crystal blue eyes, the perfect adornment for the handsome and successful Charlie Abercrombie.

"She's always been kinda wild," Mrs. Young continued. "Homer and I never did have a lot of friends. We were always content to be together. So

I've never talked about this with people from church. And now I no longer have Homer." Her eyes were the color of denim that had lost its crispness, and the woman herself seemed to follow suit. Washed in grief, she was fading.

Ruth Abercrombie let the door slam behind her as she stepped onto the patio. She was wearing pink mules and an oversized pink terry cloth robe, covering a white, frilly nightgown that stuck out at the collar. She scuffed over and plopped down in the last unoccupied plastic chair. *Here's the mess*, thought Abby.

The porcelain was gone; a rag doll remained. Her skin was muslin; her hair was mud-brown yarn. She sagged in the chair unable to sit up straight. Abby drew a hand through her own hair. Her lips failed a full smile when Mrs. Young introduced them to Ruth.

"Hi," was Ruth's flat response. She kept her eyes on the patio concrete just in front of her mother's feet.

"Your mom told us that you'd come to stay, so we thought we'd come over and invite you to a Sunday school picnic/yard sale that we are having on Saturday." Duncan exuded friendliness.

Indeed friendliness seemed to be pimpling out every pore, Abby thought wryly.

Ruth raised her eyes to Duncan's.

"Thanks. If you'll excuse me." She stood up and walked away. The door slapped shut behind her.

"I'm sorry she was rude."

"It's OK. It's obvious that something is really wrong," Abby said.

"Well, I told you that she left her husband. He

finally called here two days after she'd gone. I didn't know that she hadn't told him." She wrung her hands in her lap. "I thought that was odd."

Abby and Duncan nodded their heads in agreement with her.

"He said that she has been traveling with her job quite a bit lately, and she had a trip scheduled for the day that she showed up here. He went to meet her plane, and she wasn't there. Then he called her office. Well, you can figure that out ... " She waved away the long explanation with her hand.

"Finally he called here."

"Did she ever say why she left?"

"No. She won't tell me. She just said she needs some time. She won't even talk to Charlie. That's her husband. I offered to get the pastor if she wanted someone to talk to, but she just said no."

They all looked up when Ruth came back outside wearing blue jeans and a tee shirt. She had finger-combed her hair back into a ponytail.

"I thought maybe you would go for a walk with me?" she asked Abby.

This day just gets weirder and weirder, Abby thought. She glanced at Duncan. He nodded.

"Sure," she answered. "Where are we going?"

"Just down the block."

"If you wouldn't mind," Mrs. Young addressed herself to Duncan. "I have a light bulb in my sewing room that needs changing and I'm just getting too old to be climbing on the furniture."

Duncan stood up. "Show me the way."

The dryness of the garden was left behind.

"I know this is somewhat odd." Ruth fixed her crystal eyes on Abby. "But I felt I could talk to you."

"I'm glad to help if I can. But we don't even know each other."

"Actually, that's a good thing. I don't have any friends left. So since you are not my friend, I can't lose. You know?"

"I think so."

They began to walk down the sidewalk. Ruth kept interlocking her fingers and bending her hands back.

"I guess Mom probably told you everything."

"She told me that you left your husband, and he called here looking for you."

"Well, that's all she knows. I can't tell her the truth. You have to promise me you won't tell her."

"I won't."

They had made it to the end of the short block and crossed the street. The sidewalk in front of this house was rust colored.

"I left Charlie, that's my husband, so that I can get clean."

Ruth was rubbing her hand up and down along the inside of her arm. Abby looked for needle marks. Ruth's arm was smooth.

"Do you believe in dreams?—Abby, right?" Abby nodded, yes, that was her name.

"Do you believe in dreams?" Ruth asked again.

"Do you mean, do I think God can talk to us in our dreams?"

"Yes."

"Yes. I believe that," Abby answered.

"Mother doesn't." There it was, a hint of the

aloofness that she had experienced with Ruth before. "She believes in the Bible. She believes in miracles, but she doesn't believe that they can happen to us."

"There're lots of people who think that way. But I figure God talked to Joseph that way and Daniel and even Nebuchadnezzar, so why not me? Same spirit of God. New day," Abby responded.

"That is what I always thought, too." She spoke slowly, choosing her words carefully, as though if she just talked, her roots would show.

"You have to be careful, though. You have to know your Bible or you can get tricked," Abby said.

"I had a dream this morning. It was one of those. You know what I mean? The mist clears, and then you can see clearly? It's like you're there. And you can remember the details better than if you watched it on television."

Abby nodded.

"I dreamed that I was on a boat with you..." Ruth continued.

"With me?"

"Yes, isn't that strange?" Ruth stopped, and Abby expected a pointed look, but Ruth's eyes were settled at a point just above her head.

"Anyway"—they continued walking—"the water below us was green and swirling and we were headed toward the east."

"What else?"

"Nothing. That was it. But then I got up and came out and there you were."

Ruth stopped abruptly and put her hand up. "No, wait. We had just come through a storm and we were soaking wet."

They resumed walking, stepping down a curb, mounting the next.

"What do you think it means?" Abby asked.

"I don't know, but I think that you and I are linked somehow." They were both quiet for a few more square lengths of sidewalk.

"Why were we soaking wet? Maybe we're going to face a troubled time at the same time," Ruth went on.

"I think that because we are in the boat together, it means we go through it together," Abby ventured.

"Oh, I see."

"What did you mean that you left your husband so that you could get clean?" Abby probed.

"Do you know what it means to be sober? Really sober?" Ruth stopped again to not look Abby in the eye.

"Yeah, I think so."

"It means that you'll die before you'll ever have another drink. Even if a drink is sitting there, and you are dying to have it, and you feel like you might die if you don't have it. So be it"—she swiped the air with her hand—"you'll die. That's what I have to do: be sober."

"You don't look like an alcoholic."

"People are seldom what they seem. I'm not an alcoholic. I'm a drunk of a different type. But the principle is the same. I had to come here to get in control."

They walked quietly for a short time.

"Odd thing is," Ruth began again, "that I used to think of myself as a Christian. When I was a child, you know. But lately I haven't given it much thought. I mean Charlie and I came to church for the holidays, because it was part of the family tradition. Now here I am."

Ruth gazed at the ground. They were crossing another rusty patch of sidewalk, and Abby fleetingly wondered why it was so. Ruth was looking forward again. Abby studied the white clouds forming into huge mansions in the sky. *What kind of drunk was she? What does she need me for?*

She had become so absorbed in her thoughts that Ruth's voice startled her.

"I prayed for help yesterday. And here you are." There was a bit of awe in her voice.

"You have to hold on to that." Abby turned to Ruth to emphasize her thought. "Remember that God is not far. Even when it gets hard." Ruth searched her eyes. Abby continued, "Life is hard, and we find ourselves on paths we did not expect to travel, but He is still there." They were moving again.

"Gosh, I know that sounds really trite, but it's true. I had always thought that if you were divorced, you had screwed up badly. I mean, you could never do anything for Him again. And as I was going through my divorce"—she paused while she looked for the right words—"it's like He threw his coat over me and called me his own. He takes care of me. Always. He'll take care of you, too."

"We'd better turn around," Ruth suggested. "I don't suppose you have all day to be walking around town with me."

Indeed they had walked more than two miles, traveling past the Gordons' and winding up near the strip mall. The abrupt suggestion to change direction gave Abby a feeling that she had said the wrong thing. But she decided she had nothing else to give, and maybe this woman who couldn't share what was wrong with her needed to hear that the Lord was close and loved her just as He always loved Abby. So she pressed on.

"Do you have a Bible?" Abby asked.

"I used to. Mother probably still has it."

Abby could detect once again a separation between the two of them.

"Only God can give the interpretation of dreams." Ruth looked at her sideways. She had picked up the pace a little, her long legs taking almost a cube of sidewalk at a time. Abby took them by halves. She was beginning to get out of breath.

"It's in Daniel. You must get a Bible, and you have to study it."

They walked the rest of the way in silence. Abby's short legs took two strides to Ruth's one. In the block just before Ruth's house, Abby ventured one more idea.

"You can just read for starters, you know. It might be too much to think of studying." Abby emphasized the word, like the word itself was a burdensome tome. "Just begin reading, and He'll guide you."

Ruth smiled a tight-lipped grin with her chin slightly pointed to the sky.

"Thank you for walking with me today." Her formal tone was dismissive.

Duncan was sitting on the porch with Mrs. Young. His broad smile warmed Abby and drove from her the momentary uncertainty that Ruth's dismissive tone had caused.

"Are you ready?" he asked. His manner was as

good-natured as she had always seen it. If there was some dark thing lurking behind that smile and those warm eyes she couldn't find it.

"Thanks again for coming." Ruth turned and went into the house.

"Thanks very much." Mrs. Young addressed Abby.

"You're welcome."

The three walked to Duncan's truck. Abby and Duncan got in. Mrs. Young stood by Abby's door.

"She's been walking a lot since she came here. I wish she wouldn't walk alone." She wrung her hands.

"I think she's gonna be OK," Abby said.

Duncan leaned across Abby to speak to Mrs. Young. Abby's heart raced at his nearness.

"We have to go, Mrs. Young. Call me when that part comes in for your dryer, and I'll install it for you."

"Thank you, Duncan." She waved at them as they drove down the street.

"Well, how'd it go?" Duncan hadn't made it down to the end of the short street.

"Wait a minute." She felt like if she started talking, Mrs. Young, or even worse, Ruth, would be able to hear the whole thing.

When they had cleared the neighborhood, Abby felt a sense of relief.

"Do you believe in dreams, Duncan? The kind that tell the future or give understanding that we wouldn't have otherwise." He kept his eyes on the road. "You know, do you think that God still speaks to us in dreams?"

Just when she'd figured out that she'd said exactly the wrong thing and decided that he must think she was a kook, he spoke.

"Yes. I've had a couple of those. But you must be very cautious."

"Yes, I know. That's what I told Ruth. She had a dream this morning before we arrived and I was in it."

Duncan's eyes left the road and found Abby's.

Abby relayed to Duncan the conversation she had shared with Ruth, including the odd change in Ruth from friendly to cool on their way back.

"Oh, it's probably nothing. She probably just realized the time. You guys were gone for nearly an hour."

"Sorry."

"No, that's what we went for, but I do need to get back to the office."

"I wonder what she needed to be sober from. And if that has anything to do with why her mother's Social Security check went missing."

"Maybe she gambles."

"That would explain it. She said she wasn't an alcoholic. What were your dreams about?"

Again, Duncan was quiet, picking his words or watching the traffic. She didn't know him well enough yet to be sure.

"Nothing much. I pushed my hand through a looking glass and found myself in a very scary place. I didn't do it again."

"I have seen that place. Have you ever seen the future?"

"No."

They rode the rest of the way to the dock in silence. Abby was glad to be out of the Young house with its bizarre happenings. There was something sinister there, and according to Ruth, she was supposed to be linked with her somehow. If that were so, then how come she hadn't heard yet? Or had she because Ruth had told her?

She was reasonably sure Ruth's vision was authentic because of the green swirling water. She had seen the water many times.

The first time she had seen anything she was just a child. She had seen herself swimming in her house full of the green, swirling water. She was laughing. She could breathe under the water. She had told her mother, who said something along the lines of "That's interesting, dear," or "Neat dream." Whatever it was, she could no longer remember. Helen did not have the gift and didn't believe anyone else did either.

Her grandmother taught her about the sight; she said it ran in their family. Her mother, Abby's great-grandmother, had to be very careful not to say anything about what she had seen because people would have called her crazy and locked her up. Nowadays people would still call you crazy, but most were more likely to chase you around looking for wisdom than throw you in the nut house.

Sitting around the large rectangular table in her grandmother's dining room with mugs of steaming coffee was always the venue for these stories. Abby missed those days. She missed the fellowship with a kindred spirit.

Grandma told her about the green water. Green was the color for life. Water represented spirit. The green water was spirit life: the word of God, the life of God. That part of Ruth's vision anyway was not a fake. The rest of it she didn't know about. Were they soaking wet because He had covered them, and their life was spared?

Ruth was nobody to her. She was surely nobody to Ruth. *Was she to help her through this drunken problem of hers? How?*

The question faded when they arrived back at MacLeod Tours. Duncan disappeared into his office and Abby did not see much of him until Saturday morning at the youth yard sale.

Chapter 21

It was early enough for the sky to still glow purple and orange in the chilly air when Abby pulled her car into the church parking lot. She was just in time to see Duncan hoist a large box of goods out of the back of his pickup truck and carry them to a table. His feet left tracks in the dew-laden grass. It was hard to look away from the sight of his muscular body even when Pastor Bob came up beside her.

"Abby," he boomed, "Delia Petersen can't come, and she knows the prices for everything. Do you think you could take over tagging this stuff?"

"Sure. Come on out, Chloe." Chloe climbed across the seats to exit out the driver's door. They followed Bob over to the first of several long cafeteria-style tables. The hospitality table was loaded with a large decanter of coffee, another with hot water for tea or cocoa, and two large boxes of doughnuts. Under the table were several more boxes of doughnuts. The familiar crew of Mrs. Young, Penny, the pastor's wife, and the couple that led the youth group were busy emptying boxes onto tables and blankets for display. All the usual stuff was there: books for a dime, old records for a quarter, dishes for a nickel. It seemed a wonder that these tired objects would raise any money and yet, every year the Lord blessed their efforts for the youth on missions.

Abby rooted around on a table laden with clothes for the necessary roll of masking tape. She pulled a pen from her pocket and set to work. She was aware of Duncan on the edge of her sight. It was not unlike keeping track of Chloe. Chloe sat herself down next to a small box of children's clothes and began to help by pulling out one piece at a time and throwing it on the grass behind her back.

Abby picked up all the clothes, tossed them back into the box, taped a label with a price on the front, and put the box near a blanket display. People were arriving. Abby pulled Chloe behind the tables with her.

"They come early, don't they?" Duncan's breath tickled the nape of her neck.

Abby turned abruptly. He stepped back to avoid spilling the two cups of coffee he carried.

"Coffee?" He grinned.

"Yes, please." She took the cup from him.

"I want doughnut." Chloe clutched at Abby's waist.

"I'll get her one. Would you like one?" His brown eyes were happy and warm, unlike last time they had been together. Chloe reached up and put her hand in his.

"Can I come?" Chloe asked.

Duncan looked up at Abby. He seemed

surprised.

"Can you tell me how much this is?" A woman's gruff voice pushed in between them. She thrust a hand holding two square wooden plaques of painted flowers before their eyes.

"We'll be right back." Duncan took Chloe.

It'll be all right, she told herself. There isn't anywhere for them to go; she could see the refreshments from where she stood. Abby turned to the woman. She had bright, bottle-red hair. Her eyes were gleaming. She was ready to haggle.

"Two dollars."

"Oh." The bluster disappeared and she began to smile.

"I'll take them."

Abby took her money. She had time to look down toward the hospitality table to see Duncan pulling out doughnuts.

"Do you really want three dollars for this phone?"

A label on the top of the phone in dark black said: "$3.00 FIRM"

"Yes, sir."

"It's not worth three dollars."

"Sir, it's not my phone. I can only go by the label."

"Well, I used to work for the phone company, and I can tell ya that this phone is not worth three dollars."

Chapter 22

Duncan had never held so little a hand. Chloe's fingers were cool and soft and fragile. He was at once concerned that the callouses on the pads of his fingers would scratch the delicate surface of this little girl.

Lord, he prayed, *how do I do this?*

Chloe looked up at him and smiled as if she heard his prayer. She slipped in the dewy grass, and he held her up with his arm. She giggled as she dangled from his hand.

"What kind of doughnut do you want?"

The hospitality table was loaded down with the best cakes, cookies, muffins, and even strudel that Ocean View had to offer. It was all for sale, except for the doughnuts that had been provided expressly for the volunteer workers.

"Sprinkles."

Duncan let go of Chloe long enough to reach around to the back of the coffee pot to retrieve the pastry. Chloe got the last sprinkled one. The woman who wanted the plaques was gone, and now Abby was talking to an older man holding a phone. With Chloe's hand in his he walked them back toward Abby, then veered off to the right into the parking lot toward his truck. He dropped the tailgate and he and Chloe sat there, feet dangling, eating doughnuts.

Chapter 23

Abby's heart ached watching Chloe and Duncan laughing and swinging their feet over the lowered tailgate of Duncan's truck. *Why couldn't that be Chloe's father she's having fun with this morning?*

She realized then that she had not seen Brad or heard from him in two weeks. Which suited her just fine. She was still furious that he had come on to her that night.

"Excuse me, are these really twenty-five cents?" A sharp blonde woman was holding up a few sleeper nighties. "I usually pay ten cents for them. I get them for my church."

"Ten cents is fine," Abby said.

The rest of the morning continued in the same way: haggling over pennies, drinking coffee, and eating doughnuts. By early afternoon, Abby decided it was time to pack up Chloe and go home. She headed toward Duncan who was pushing Chloe on the swings.

"Thank you for watching Chloe this morning. I can't tell you how much I appreciated it."

"You're welcome. She's a wonderful little girl."

"I think so." She smiled at him. "Come on, Chloe. It's time to go."

Even the child seemed to sense the need to go. She came quietly to her mother's side.

Duncan stretched his arms to the sky and yawned.

"Would you mind some company?"

Abby squashed the words of her mother in her mind. She was too tired to be wary. Besides, how could she say no? He had done her a huge favor by watching Chloe all morning.

"Sure. Come on."

They walked together toward the parking lot. The quiet of the drive revived Abby. By the time she was home, she was ready to make lunch and go for a walk. She could put Chloe in the stroller. She was growing out of her stroller, but Abby could get away with it every once in a while. And she knew Chloe would go right to sleep after the morning's activities. Besides, it would give them something to do. Maybe the exercise would help defuse the electricity sparking between her and Duncan.

She made tuna on rye and served iced tea. After lunch she fished out the stroller and off they went in the direction of the beach. Chloe was asleep before they turned the first corner.

The shops on River Road were still shut down for winter. Most would open up after Memorial Day. They walked along a sidewalk made wavy with time. Sand filled the cracks and odd joints. Chloe slept through the swells and dips of her stroller ride.

There was a cool spring breeze coming off the Bay. The trees were studded with bright green leaves. The azaleas were blooming pink and white in yards they passed.

"I forgot how much I loved it here," Duncan said.

"I'm not sure I did love it until I came back to it," Abby replied.

"I'm not sure I did either. But it's good to be home again."

The little piece of yellow plaid that he always wore in his pocket flapped in the breeze.

"What is that?" Abby pointed to the scrap.

"Oh." Duncan smiled and said with a broguish lilt, "It's me tartan, lass. No laird runs around without his tartan."

Abby laughed.

"OK, what's a laird?"

"It's like a chieftain. Ruler of the tribe."

"Is it a Scottish thing then?"

"Yeah, my family came over here in the 1740's or so, and they've kept up some of the old ways."

"And that's what you are—laird? Laird Duncan MacLeod."

"Sounds old fashioned, doesn't it?"

"Not really. Lots of families have hierarchy and stuff like that."

He smiled at her then, and her breath was gone into the breeze. She could see him standing before her a great warrior dressed in tartan. Bagpipes seemed to whisper in the wind. They turned away from the Bay and went back toward home.

"So the man who came the first day I met you and picked up Chloe... I assume he's her father?"

"Yes, he's my ex-husband."

"What happened?"

Abby explained briefly that she and Brad were living out of state when they met Suzie. Suzie and Abby had been friends; then Brad and Suzie left together.

"Does he live here then?"

"No. He's being transferred here. He works in computers. It's strange that he's back." She felt it wise not to tell him that Brad had asked her to get back together with him that first night.

"He says he wants to see Chloe, but he hasn't seen her in two weeks. I'm not even sure he's still in town."

They were passing the Gordons' house. Pat waved from the picture window.

"Hi, Pat!" Abby spoke softly, but waved enthusiastically. She hoped the enthusiasm would communicate to her friend.

"You know them?" Duncan's face was guarded. A cloud crossed his features.

"Yes. I'm a hospice volunteer. How do you know them?"

"It's not them. I was friends with their son, Max, in high school. Is it the old man?"

Is that it? A high school prank maybe? Was that the big tragedy that has people up in arms about Duncan?

"Yes. Do you still keep up with him—the son?"

"Yes, he's a missionary in Ecuador right now."

"I knew that he was out of the country, but Pat

hasn't told me what he does."

"Tell me more about Brad."

"There isn't much to say. He's a creep. I struggle with Chloe needing to see him because he's her father."

They walked the rest of the way home in silence. The sidewalk was small, and one or the other of them had to keep slightly ahead. They alternated based on the sidewalk waves. Chloe was still asleep when they reached her door.

Duncan stepped up to Abby and leaned in to hug her, his hands on her waist.

"I had a wonderful time today. Thank you."

Abby's heart was pounding. She reached up and put her arms around him but stopped on his biceps.

"Me, too" was all she could manage to say, with him so close, their bodies nearly touching. The desire she had been suppressing for days surfaced all at once and she wanted him to kiss her again. This time for real. Her body softened in response to the feel of his arms encasing her, and she leaned toward him. He held her close for a fraction of a heartbeat, long enough to feel the curve of her body fit into his. He quickly stiffened and he put distance between them.

"I'll see you in the morning." He smiled at her again.

Rebuffed, Abby resisted the urge to invite him in for dinner. Flustered, she watched him walk back to his car, get in and drive away.

She tried to console herself that she was glad that he had pushed her away. In fact, he had actually saved the day. If he had responded to her the way she had wanted him to, she knew she wouldn't have been able to stop herself. And then where would she be?

She already knew she wasn't supposed to be involved with Duncan MacLeod. She had been warned by those she trusted; and she had seen the cloud cross Duncan's face.

What had he done? How did it involve Max Gordon? Maybe she could ask Pat when she went there next.

The cool spring breeze blew the days by quickly. Saturday fluttered into Sunday and on to Wednesday without any trouble. Abby kept herself busy at work doing odd jobs, copying, and answering the phone. On Tuesday, she kept an appointment with Jack to learn to use a propane stove.

Jack was playing a merry sea chanty on his harmonica when she saw Duncan cross the parking lot in his suit and yellow tie. Her heart picked up the pace. He walked briskly with a purpose, and she could see the warrior within him. At once she had a vision of how he would look in a tartan of yellow plaid, the strong, powerful shoulders and his thick, manly legs bared for the wearing of the kilt. Jack called her back to reality with his laughter.

"So, you've got an eye for the MacLeod."

Her face warmed with a blush, but she thought it best to say nothing. After the lesson, she went back indoors to work.

Duncan popped his head into her office.

"Abby, come with me."

He waited for her in the hallway.

"It's here." His face looked like Christmas

morning. He grabbed her hand and pulled her along with him. They hopped into his truck and traveled down the road to a nearby marina. As they stepped onto the gravel parking lot, they could already see her. She was still out in the channel.

"I didn't know it was coming by water—I thought it would come by truck."

His eyes were filled with excitement. The lines of his body alive with a tension she could feel. He couldn't wait to get his hands on his new toy. She could picture him climbing in the rigging and sticking his nose into every storage bin and spinning the steering wheel.

The wind mirrored Duncan's energy: neither could keep still. It ruffled Abby's skirt, then left it alone to pick up tendrils of hair to tickle her face. She pulled it back and tied it with an elastic she had in her pocket.

The large ship seemed to grow as it glided closer and closer toward them.

It had two tall sails full of the same cool wind that blew through Abby's hair. It was painted white and blue. The sails were white with large black numbers painted on the sides. She was long and slim. Her sleek design was accented by having a long wooden bowsprit. Topside, her ornaments were lacquered wood, with railings of polished metal. One of the men on board seemed to be struggling with a large, brightly colored cloth.

Duncan and Abby walked out to the end of the dock that bounced and swayed as they went. She held onto the pilings one by one as she went down to the very end. Boats on either side of them pulled back and forth against their moorings. They stood and watched as the two men lowered the sails and strapped them down with bungee cords. They pulled up to the floating dock using a motor.

A dark-haired man tossed Duncan the rear dock lines, and a fair-haired man tossed the bow lines to Abby. Duncan tied off his by wrapping the ends around a piling and then came to Abby. Once the boat was secure, the two men came ashore.

"Duncan MacLeod." Duncan extended his hand to the dark-haired man.

"Yessir. Would you like to check her out?"

The dark-haired man appeared to be in charge. He looked like an Ivy Leaguer from the '30s. He was dressed in white pants and a white polo shirt with a golden anchor on the pocket; his white Ked's had navy blue trim. The only thing missing was the captain's hat.

The fair-haired man stood off to the side admiring the sloop.

"Yes, I do," said Duncan. In one swift movement, he was aboard and reaching his hand to Abby. Past the electricity, Abby felt the callouses on Duncan's fingers.

The boat was a sight more steady than the dock had been. Abby was glad to be on the deck.

They stepped across the narrow walkway down to the cockpit. The wood glowed in the sun. The cockpit was a small square of space with a steering wheel that reminded Abby of old Spanish galleons. White seats of molded fiberglass encircled the area. Abby knew that some, if not all, would open to reveal storage below.

Toward the center of the ship was the opening for below decks. Down below was dark compared to the blinding white cockpit. The air in the cabin was warm. The men must have run the heater in the cool morning, Abby thought. Once her eyes adjusted, she found herself in a narrow walkway. Duncan bumped into her from behind; Abby felt ripples of desire in response. She turned and looked up at him; he smiled. Did he know the effect he was having on her?

She made her way quickly into the main room of the cabin. *Get a grip*, she told herself: *wrong time, wrong place.* But it wasn't going to be easy; the closeness of the cabin made the large craft feel more like a dingy.

Duncan called her attention to a closet-like opening on the left side of the hallway that turned out to be a bathroom, complete with a shower. Across from there, on the right, was a small kitchen.

Inside was all golden varnished wood and white walls that reminded Abby of beamed ceilings and stucco walls. Small rectangular windows ran at Abby's eye level throughout the cabin. The narrow hallway that housed the kitchen opened into a living space. On the wall was a small chrome heater that looked like a miniature pot-bellied stove. There were more of the molded seats covered with dark blue microfiber cushions and more storage underneath.

Beyond the room was a door that led to the V-berth. Filling just about that whole space was a bed. There were more windows in there as well. The closet turned out to be another bathroom, but the ceiling was not as high as the first one she had seen. No doubt this was where the guests would sleep.

Abby was getting excited. It would be a wonderful adventure to travel in such a vessel.

"What do you think?" The question felt intimate in the small room. Duncan's brown eyes twinkled with excitement; Abby imagined she could feel his heart beat through the three feet of air that was between them.

"It's beautiful."

"We'll need to do some fixing up and customizing. I want you to take these cushions to the upholstery shop and have them make up nicer ones. Shall we?" He motioned for her to procede topside with him.

Abby slipped by him, careful not to graze his arm. She tingled when he put his hand into the small of her back.

On deck, the two men were waiting. The dark-haired man stepped up to the railing. The fair-haired man walked off down the dock.

"Well, whatcha think?"

"I'll take it."

"Good. Now I have a few things to show ya, before we leave."

The man boarded and took Duncan through the mechanics of the freezer, which he assured them, "Ain't the same as the refrigerator you got at home."

Abby sat in the cockpit and listened to the water lapping at the sides trying to get a grip on her feelings for Duncan MacLeod. Just then, she had the feeling that she had been here before. Just on the edge of her memory was the dream. She had the sense of it; she stood on a boat above the swirling green water headed to the east. Ahead was a large white storm.

She couldn't place Ruth there. What had she to do with Abby? Was she on the other side of the storm? Or were they not connected at all? Ruth had come to the youth yard sale. Abby had seen her briefly. She must have dropped off items for the sale. She didn't stay long enough to talk to Abby.

After nearly an hour, Duncan signed the necessary papers that said he had received his boat. Then Captain Smith and his sidekick packed their small bags and were gone.

"You ready?" Duncan was exhilarated. His excitement animated the smallest movements. Abby didn't think he could keep still if his life depended on it. All the same she felt useless while Duncan scrambled around securing lines and straightening the sails. They pulled away from the dock smoothly. Once they were in the channel, Duncan raised the sails and sat down in the cockpit. Abby stood next to him taking in all she could. The feeling that she belonged here with him was overwhelming. *It's too comfortable*, she thought. She was going to have to fight her heart on this one.

They had gone down the channel for a short distance, and Duncan had turned and headed toward the MacLeod's dock before Abby voiced her nagging thought.

"Do you think Mrs. Young is OK ... I mean financially? Should we bring her meals? I forgot to ask her that when we went over the other day."

"She's OK. The Social Security people will reissue the check once they figure out that it's not her signature."

"She'll probably have the next check by then. What is she supposed to do in the meantime?"

"She's OK. Can you steer this for a minute? I want to fix something."

Abby watched Duncan walk up to the bow and wriggle one of the ropes loose. Then she knew. He had given Mrs. Young the money she needed. He just didn't want to talk about it. She smiled.

"What do you make of Ruth?"

"I don't know yet." He sat down beside her again taking over the wheel. He corrected their heading slightly.

"I do know this: that when you have something out of whack like an addiction, you have to choose to make it right. You don't get there 'cause anyone did it for you." His eyes were focused ahead. He squinted at something in the distance. "The only thing God ever asked us to do is choose our salvation. You've got to choose it."

The dock came into clear view. Before they turned in, Duncan got up and dropped the sails. Abby held their course. Duncan steered the boat under motor power toward the dock. As they came closer, Andrew and Angus came out of the building to assist them.

Angus and Andrew were as excited as their brother had been and quickly became lost in the belly of the boat once she was safely docked. They called to one another as they made their assessments.

Abby excused herself and headed toward her car. Duncan caught up with her halfway across the parking lot.

"Will you give me a ride to the dock so I can pick up my truck?"

Abby felt the color drain from her face. Duncan in her car? She panicked. When was the last time she cleaned it? She couldn't remember when she last moved the car seat to make room for an adult. Who knew what was under there?

"Sure. Just give me a second to move the car

seat." She smiled hoping it didn't look like a cringe.

She hoped the picture of the new boat sitting at his dock would distract him. Instead he followed her right over to her little yellow car. He turned to gaze at the boat.

She got right to work. Mercifully the interior was black. She unclipped the seatbelt that held the car seat in place. It hung limply where she placed it instead of retracting. She pulled the belt and crumbs fell onto the seat and tumbled to the floor. She reached with both hands to remove the car seat, which wouldn't budge.

With a little effort she was able to break the suction seal that had formed around the car seat from the seat itself. There she found old French-fries and crumbs and other bits and pieces from unidentifiable sources. She grabbed the closest napkin she could find and began flinging the bits of fries and other detritus on to the parking lot. A sharp movement caught her eye, but not fast enough to stop the load of particles from hitting Duncan's legs. She felt her face flame with embarrassment.

"Oh, I am so sorry!" She squelched her first instinct, which was to run over and brush him off with the napkin she had shredded trying to get the seat clean. Instead she just stood there helplessly while Duncan brushed himself off.

"It's all right." He looked up and smiled at her.

Her heart skipped a beat. She turned back to the seat and wiped it down with a wet-nap.

His shadow loomed over her. "Got any more fries in there? I'm starving."

She rolled her eyes at him as she stood up, and there they were again—much too close. "No, I think that about does it for the fries." She pushed past him, went around to the driver's side, and got in.

Duncan barely fit in the front seat of Abby's little car. He adjusted the seat, strapped himself in and started to laugh.

Chapter 24

Duncan leaned against his truck and watched Abby drive away. A laugh from deep inside erupted. It was slow coming on, but now he knew she was the one. It was the fries under the seat that got him. He would have been out of the way if he hadn't been following so close. He had paid no attention to where they were going. He had been thinking of what a night onboard his new boat with her would be like. There was no one in the world like her, no one that made him feel this way. *You have to be careful what you ask for*, he told himself, *you just might get it*. He drove on autopilot as Abby filled his thoughts.

Passing the Gordons' house brought him out of his reverie. Oswald Gordon. Sour old man. He would have to try again. He owed it to his father, Mr. Gordon and Max. Perhaps Gordon would listen to him this time. Perhaps he could forgive before he died. He would call. His mother probably still had the number. She had been friends with Pat Gordon for years before the incident. He would call first to ask permission, and then he would go see the old man.

He kicked himself again for the damage he had done to his family. How painful it must have been for his mother to be separated from her friend because of him. If he had learned the lesson from this first big mistake, John never would have died.

Max and Duncan had been fast friends since kindergarten. It helped that Ossy worked for Duncan's father at the dock. The boys were thrown together at school and at church. They did everything together: they were acolytes, they rode bikes, they raced against each other in the soap box derby. Then, at seventeen, in their senior year of high school, they went out in Ossy Gordon's car with a baseball bat and booze. Joy riding and bashing in as many mailboxes as they could get away with had become their new hobby.

It was the third Saturday night of their spree. Max was driving. Duncan was hanging out of the window. They were driving fast down Longstreet, a winding rural road. They had hit six mailboxes by the time they reached Hermit Hogan's.

Hermit Hogan lived on a dirt farm littered with falling barns and an old homestead going to seed. Hogan never came out except to feed his dogs and go to the grocery store. He had a big red mailbox ripe for picking.

He must have heard them coming on that quiet rural road where you can hear your neighbor gossiping a mile down if the wind is still. Duncan's arms were still ringing from the first six he'd smashed when they came up on Hermit's. Duncan hung out the window, bat at the ready. Before he could swing, a shot pinged off the top of the car. Duncan ducked inside.

"Go! He's shootin' at us—" Max drove up to the next driveway and backed up and went back to Hermit's.

"What are you doin'?!"

Hogan was still on his porch, standing in the yellow light of a bug bulb, peering into the night, the shotgun at rest in the crook of his arm. Max got out and put his hands up in the air, in surrender. Hogan shot him. Max hit the ground. The top of his arm was torn off. Duncan belly-crawled to the driver's-side door. Hogan was still shooting. Duncan grabbed Max by the belt buckle and pulled him into the car. Once Max was inside Duncan peeled out of there and drove straight to the hospital. The police were called from there.

Max lost the use of his left arm forever, and Ossy Gordon held Duncan responsible for the ruination of his son's life. If Duncan had not talked Max into it, good little Max would never have been harmed. Max knew otherwise.

He and Duncan remained friends, but Max changed the course of his life. He figured he could have died that night and the Lord must have wanted him alive. So he got training, and after college, he went off to Ecuador as a missionary. They hadn't seen each other since high school graduation, but that was going to change soon. Max was getting married in a couple of months and he was coming home on furlough.

Chapter 25

Abby lay in her bed Wednesday night full of dread. She had fallen for Duncan MacLeod. Tomorrow she would start avoiding him at all costs. No more walks; no more lunches on the bench outside. She pictured him walking with her and holding her hand. They had laughed and talked. She laughed again at the sound of his brogue.

"'Tis me tartan, lass..."

She couldn't remember a time like that with Brad. He was always on about the way things looked. What people thought. How he was going to get ahead. Her elation began to fade, so she turned her thoughts back to Duncan. But the pure joy was lost. He and Chloe on the back of his truck dangling their legs. He seemed to understand that it was simple to love a child. They only want your attention...and a little time.

She would have to find a new job. She couldn't possibly work that closely with him and stay away. On the other hand, the benefits were good, and she had no other prospect at hand. She would just have to steel herself. Obviously he liked her a little. She would just have to make sure that it didn't go any further.

She wondered if her mother had found out anything. Maybe there was no deep, sinister past, and Helen had gotten the whole thing mixed up with someone else. After all, it had been a long time ago. Maybe this would all clear up for the best, and her heart was on the right track. Maybe the best was that she and Duncan would be married and live happily ever after.

Not likely, she told herself.

She drifted to sleep dreaming of different scenarios where Duncan was exonerated leaving him free for her.

Her mind worked so tirelessly at the task that she did not realize she had fallen asleep. A loud pounding on the door woke her. The big red numbers on her clock said 3:00 a.m. She hesitated. If it was Brad, she wasn't letting him in. Wrapping a robe around herself, she went to the door.

"Who is it?" She spoke through the wooden door. She was glad that the grids were secure on her windows.

"It's me—Ruth."

Abby looked through the peephole. It *was* Ruth. She looked out the window. There was no one else there, so she opened the door. The glass was between them.

"I'm so afraid," Ruth said. She was back to the rag doll look. Her skin was the color of white muslin in the porch light.

"Come in, but please keep your voice down. My daughter is sleeping."

Ruth came in and looked around the room with her chin in the air. Abby was in no mood. She stepped into the hall and closed Chloe's door. She had to give up Duncan; she wasn't going to give up sleep.

Tears dripped down Ruth's face.

"What's going on?"

"This is so hard." She took a deep breath.

Abby waited. They were both standing in her kitchen. Abby felt her compassion kick in.

So much for sleep, she thought. *Lord give me wisdom*, she prayed.

"Have a seat. Want some tea?" she asked. Abby got down a box of tissues from the top of the fridge. Ruth pulled out a chair and sat down. She rested her hands in her lap.

"No, thank you."

Abby put water on to boil. She could use some tea.

"So what are you afraid of?" Abby sat across from Ruth with a steaming cup.

"I'm an addict." Ruth began to pull on her fingers.

She seemed to expect some kind of reaction, so Abby said, "OK."

"I'm so filthy. I was trying to pray. Trying to talk to Charlie. I can't. I have been going to every meeting that I can find. I can't—" Her eyes welled up again rendering her speechless.

Abby reached over and took one of her hands. Ruth pulled back.

"You don't understand—"

"I'll wait until you can tell me." Abby gently

rested back in her chair.

"They told us that we shouldn't... " Ruth hiccupped through another bout of tears. "Shouldn't... "

Abby waited. Ruth took a deep breath and began again.

"They told us that we shouldn't tell our families what we do. It's too gross for normal people—"

She dabbed her eyes, "I thought maybe if I could talk to you then maybe I could get through this. I'm all alone."

"I am right here."

"I can't get my life back."

"What do you mean? Doesn't Charlie want you?"

"Yes." Ruth looked above Abby's head, focusing on something inward.

"What have you done that's so bad? Stole a check from your mother?"

"What? No—I didn't steal anything." Ruth got quiet. She turned her eyes downward to her hands.

"What is it then?"

"I'm a sex addict."

Abby stopped cold. *A what? Is this another so-called illness of the twenty-first century?*

Her spirit told her, *Listen.*

"That's why I left Charlie and came to Mother's. I couldn't do it anymore. At the program they told us not to tell our families what we've done until we've been sober for a while. Make a good track record, you know. It's too disgusting for normal people. That's why I came here. I'm so alone. I need a real Christian to talk to. I know that you are the real thing. You and that boyfriend of yours."

"What is a sex addict?"

"It's like being an alcoholic. I have to have it."

Abby's skepticism began to wane. "So you can't just stop?"

"I don't know. I have done such awful things."

"Like what?" Abby wasn't sure she really wanted to know.

"I was OK for a little while after I was married to Charlie. But then I just needed to have a fix, you know. I went out with a guy in my office for a little while. But he got too serious, so I broke it off. Then there was another.

"Finally, I wound up going downtown. I met some men down there. They wanted what I wanted. No strings. No names. I thought I was OK." She took a deep breath. "I could just slip down there, and no one would be the wiser. There was even this woman one time." A new wave of choking tears clogged up her speech.

"A couple of weeks ago I went down at lunchtime, like I had been doing. I met someone I knew. He was from high school, only now he's a company executive. He knows I'm married to Charlie. I can't live like this. Charlie has talked about running for office. I can't...ruin..." Tears took over once again.

Abby waited for Ruth to finish and waited for God to give her some words.

"I've started this program before..."

"So that's what you meant by being sober?"

Ruth nodded adamantly.

Abby got up and put her cold tea in the

microwave to warm. Ruth seemed to be calming down a little. She retrieved another cup from the cabinet and made her a cup of tea as well.

"First, I have to tell you that you are not too gross for God. Jesus covered all that with His sacrifice. Have you ever thought of what a physically brutal death Jesus suffered? "

"Well, I don't think I ever imagined what it would be like to be nailed down, if that's what you mean."

"I hadn't either until recently when I was reading Luke. It says Jesus was in agony as he prayed in the garden His sweat became like drops of blood. When I get nervous, I get cramps. It makes me think of that. He knew how hard it would be, but He did it for you." She paused for a sip of tea; Ruth's gaze never left her.

"You know there aren't any deep, black sins and pale, white sins," she continued. "Sin is sin. Oh and by the way, He had to die for me, too." She noticed her Bible sitting on the table where she left it. "Were you able to find your Bible?"

"Yes, Mother still had it."

"Have you ever read the book of Ruth?"

"That's the one about the woman who becomes queen?"

"No, that's Esther. Ruth is one of my favorites because it's so romantic."

"I really don't think—"

"I don't mean in a sexual kind of way." Abby hesitated, but in her spirit she knew she was right on track. "You will have to bear with me. I don't mean to be preachy..." she continued.

"Ruth was from Moab. She would have been

the equivalent of a pagan today. She was married to a guy from Israel. After he died, she went back to Israel with her mother-in-law. Leaving the pagans she came from, she chose the God of Israel for herself. Once in Israel, she went to a relative's farm to glean."

"Why?" Ruth asked.

"Because that was how they fed the widows and the orphans. The owner of the field was called Boaz. When Ruth meets Boaz, he tells her that she may eat and drink of the food and water he has provided for his household. Then he tells the workers that they are to harvest some and leave enough for Ruth to glean. Throughout the harvest time he looks out for Ruth. Eventually, she goes to him and he marries her."

Ruth remained silent.

"The reason I love it so much is because Boaz is Jesus. You are Ruth. He loves you. He doesn't care where you come from or what you've been into. He loves you, and He forgives you."

"It's so hard."

"I know it is, but you can do it with the strength of Christ. Rely on it. I will be here to help you. Call me anytime. Just do what you have to do."

"I have to call Charlie."

"Do you want to call him now?"

"No. I'll wait. Do you think it's OK not to tell him everything right now?"

"You have to figure that out for yourself. But you do have to go to your meetings. Do what they tell you. You should come to church. You can't go back downtown."

Light began to filter through the blinds. The

cups of tea sat cold.

"It's daylight," Abby yawned.

"Oh, don't do tha—" Ruth let loose a large one of her own.

"I have to get ready for work."

"I'm sorry."

"It's OK. You can call me anytime."

It was five thirty by the time Abby gave Ruth a hug and closed the door behind her. It would not be wise for her to lie down at all. Instead, Abby got in the shower. It was going to be a long day.

At least now that the boat was in, she would have some real work to do. She would drop off the cushions and buy some towels and other things. If she had to, she would make up odd jobs or someone might just find her asleep in a corner somewhere. Duncan had already chosen the fabric, so that made quick work at the upholsterer. She was able to get a swatch and that helped with the task of finding the matches for the other things. She bought thick, oversized towels for the V-berth and a couple of terry cloth robes, pillows and travel-sized toothbrushes and toothpaste for anyone who came without. Myriad other little details consumed the rest of her day. She arrived home with Chloe exhausted and looked forward to an early bedtime.

At seven thirty the phone rang.

It was Pat Gordon.

"Abby, I've got to take Ossy to the hospital. He's having chest pains." The panic in her voice awakened Abby.

"I'll be there."

She called Helen who said she would gladly take Chloe. Grabbed her hospital identification card, and off she went to the emergency room.

Abby wasn't sure if it was dread or fatigue that caused her feet to drag through the retractable doors of the emergency room. The room was quiet except for a news channel playing on a television suspended from the wall.

She flashed her badge at the triage nurse and asked where Ossy Gordon was.

"Bed three."

Ossy was sitting up on a gurney wearing a hospital gown and had a blue crocheted blanket across his legs. Pat stood next to the bed holding his hand.

"Abby, you came," Pat said with weary smile.

"My ticker's beatin' funny, Ab. This might be it."

His eyes pierced her own, searching. Abby broke his gaze and stepped up to the foot of the bed.

"Oh, you'll be all right, Ossy. Today's not your day."

"The doctor said it's a-something fib." Pat's voice did not betray her fear, but her eyes did.

"So you've seen him already. That's good." Abby reached for Pat's hand.

"Seems they're not too busy."

"They are going to use that electric machine to give him a jolt, and that is supposed to fix the irregular beat."

The doctor, flanked by a couple of nurses, wheeled in a large machine with gray plastic paddles.

Ossy's eyes filled with tears as he sought Pat.

Abby backed out of the room. The force of Ossy's fear had startled her. She had only seen one death. A woman. But she had not been coherent. She had just slipped away. Ossy was fighting with everything God gave him to live.

"Ready."

Abby heard the machine give its jolt.

Ossy had once been a little boy running around in Boy Scout pants catching frogs. He had worked hard and raised a family. Abby had seen pictures of Max and Martha. Ossy wasn't ready to die. Not like the old woman.

Abby wiped the tears from her cheeks and took a deep breath. She was so tired.

"Looks like that did it," she heard the doctor say.

Chapter 26

Duncan climbed the old steps to Mr. and Mrs. Gordon's house. It had been a long time since he had been there. The wooden door stood open and friendly as it always was during the day when he was growing up. The windows were open; Miss Pat was letting in the fresh air. Some things didn't change. He noticed the red paint smear, where he and Max had painted their pinewood derby cars, was still visible on the middle step on the left side.

Pat had told him he could come for a few minutes, when he had called that morning. He was not allowed to upset Ossy.

"Maybe I shouldn't come. If he's too sick, it may be too late."

"Too late for whom, Duncan? He needs to see you as much as you need to see him. You come."

"I'll come."

The screen door opened as he reached the top step.

"Hello, Duncan MacLeod." She smiled politely. He felt sorry for missing the many times he had plowed into her soft middle. He stood in the small hallway. Nothing had changed but the smell. The good smell of Miss Pat's cooking was replaced by the smell of medicine. Down the hall, in the doorway of the kitchen, Duncan saw a woman in hospital scrubs.

"She's the nurse. He's in there."

Miss Pat showed the way with a sweep of her left arm.

He could feel her presence in the doorway as he approached the old man. He lay with eyes closed on a hospital bed that took up the whole room.

Duncan looked back at Miss Pat who waved him forward.

"Mr. Gordon?"

Ossy's eyes fluttered open. He must have been sleeping hard because he was disoriented when he woke.

"Mr. Gordon?"

"Who are ya? What'd'ya want?" He searched the room with his eyes. They rested on his wife just behind Duncan.

"Pat?"

"You remember Duncan MacLeod."Duncan stiffened for the old man's response.

"What do you want, MacLeod?"

"I've come to make peace with you."

"There's no peace to be made here. You're a louse, and you know it." He pointed his thumb at Duncan.

"Sir, I know that I was wrong that night. I apologize for my part—"

"So you admit it! It was your fault. You did that to your best friend. My son. He was going to go in the Army. Did you know that? He wanted to fly helicopters. Did you know that? All that was gone that night. Stole by you and your reckless behavior. Even your father knew what a waste you were." He rested back on the bed. Duncan felt the stab wound his heart.

"I hope that you can forgive me."

"Why didn't you come before?"

"I was afraid, sir. And then I was away in the Army. I didn't know you were so sick. I would have come sooner."

"Afraid of what?" Ossy was clearly disgusted at the idea.

"I don't know, sir. It all happened so fast. We were just out for some fun."

"Some fun." Ossy no longer looked at Duncan. He was looking out the window.

"You're right there, sir."

"So now you've come to ease your conscience on an old man before he dies, is that it?"

"Yes, sir."

"Army teach you that?"

"What?"

"Honesty."

"No, sir. My father did."

Duncan's heart began to twist and swell. This old man was not going to forgive him, not ever. For a time in his life, the two men—Ossy and his father—had blended in his life as one. Well, at least he had tried; now all that was left was to stand here and take whatever he had to dish out. He owed him that. He fought down the emotion that threatened to spill.

"He was a good man, Duncan."

"Yes, sir."

"You broke his heart." Ossy turned back to him again. "You don't hold it against him that he sent you away?" Ossy continued.

"No, sir I don't. He did the right thing. It's not always easy to do that."

Duncan would not allow his gaze to leave Mr. Gordon's.

"I'm gonna die, Duncan." He heard Pat's intake of breath.

"Yes, sir."

"Max doesn't live here anymore. He's off gallivantin' around the world as a missionary."

Duncan was relieved to see that he was proud of his son.

"Martha moved to Ladysmith. But you're gonna live here, ain'tcha?" Pat left the doorway and made her way softly down the hallway toward the back of the house. Relief began to course through his muscles easing the tension out of them. He was forgiven.

"Yes, sir. MacLeod Tours is mine."

"I want'cha to look out for Pat. We got no more family around here."

"Yes, sir. I will do that."

"She'll show you where the strongbox is; she's never had a head for that stuff. I've left her well provided for. But she'll need help with it."

"I'll do that, sir." Ossy slumped back on his pillow, waved Duncan away with his left hand, and closed his eyes.

Chapter 27

Abby got the call Saturday night that Ossy had died at eleven that morning. Martha had come over from Ladysmith with her family to stay with Pat. The funeral was Tuesday morning.

Abby had no trouble getting off work for the funeral because Duncan closed the doors in honor of their lifelong employee.

It was a chilly, overcast day of fog and mist. Ossy was to be buried in the Bethel graveyard, which sat atop a small hill. From the hill, the Bay was visible when the weather was clear. Today they seemed to be standing on a cliff surrounded by clouds. Under the canopy at the grave site, on a row of metal folding chairs, sat Pat in a green plaid skirt, with her daughter, Martha, to her right. Next to Martha was her husband. Abby knew them from the pictures Pat had of them on the wall.

Next to Pat on the left, was a tall straight-backed woman dressed in a yellow plaid skirt. Her long hair was piled up on top of her head. Abby gauged that she must be Erin MacLeod, Pat's friend. She must be related to Duncan; the resemblance was unmistakable. They did not share the same coloring, but you couldn't mistake the face. She should have put that together before.

He was everywhere she turned. How was she ever going to stay away from him?

Behind them were slews of people in yellow, and green and red plaids.

Abby made her way to the back of the large group. The plaintive sound of the bagpipes began. "Amazing Grace." Andrew was playing. She could see him standing off in the distance. He was so far that the song sounded like a memory in the mist.

She felt the tears well up in her eyes. How hard it must be for Pat, to have loved someone for so long and then to lose him. To be left all alone. She was going to miss Ossy herself. He was a forceful personality, and she had liked him.

Before the service began Duncan appeared at her side. The sight of him in a kilt took her breath away. Beside her stood the warrior she had seen only with her imagination. He stood uncomfortably close.

"Are you OK?"

"No, but I will be."

He put his arm around her. She was a little startled by the move, but comforted. Instead of pulling away as she knew she should, she leaned into him. His arms were strong, and she had been through so much lately. She had to stand through the service, and he stayed with her. After a short time, he let go of her, and they stood together.

When the service was over, Andrew piped the haunting sound into the mist:

"Amazing Grace, How sweet the sound..."

After the graveside service Pat opened her house for friends and family. Abby drove to the Gordons' behind Duncan. She was glad he had been there. He made her think of Boaz providing for Ruth, giving her his protection.

Pat moved through the chattering people like a ghost. She smiled here and there, but she didn't cry. Erin MacLeod ran the kitchen. She had taken off her jacket and put an apron over her kilt. She kept the trays full of folded meat and cubed cheese. She refilled drinks. Strands of hair were making their way free from her coif.

"Can I help?" Abby pulled an apron from the drawer where Pat kept them and tied it on.

"Are you Abby?"

"Yes. How did you know?"

"Well, you're the only one in here helping, and you have a fine head of brown hair. Pat has told me how good you have been to Ossy. We have been friends for many years. I am Erin MacLeod." She stuck out her hand and clasped Abby's in both of hers.

"So tell me: how do you know my Duncan?"

Chapter 28

"I work for him," Abby replied.

"I see." Erin's shrewd eyes gave her the once over.

Abby thought she probably saw more than Abby wanted her to see. Abby broke her gaze by looking around the counters for something to occupy her hands.

"Why don't you make the coffee, and I'll go check on the platters out there? We were getting low on biscuits the last time I checked," Erin said as if reading her mind, then was gone.

Abby filled the pot with water before Erin returned. Erin returned to grab a bag of rolls and scooted back out to the table. She heard Martha stop her and thank her for helping. Abby pushed the button on the coffee pot to start the brew when Duncan came in carrying two plates with rolls piled high with ham, a couple of forks of potato salad, one or two meatballs, and a few pretzels stuck on top.

"I hope you like this stuff. I figured I better get you something or you wouldn't get any."

"Thank you."

Abby took the plate from him and laid it on the counter next to her. She didn't feel like eating, but she pulled apart a roll and began to nibble politely. Her eyes brimmed with tears."

"I won't bring you food if it's gonna make you cry."

"No, it's not that."

She tried to control the quaver in her voice. How could she tell him about the wrenching time she'd been through? It wasn't just that Ossy was gone. Ossy's death had opened the floodgates of her grief—grief that her marriage failed; grief that she couldn't start over; grief that she was falling in love with him and could never have him.

"It's just—I didn't want him to die."

"I know what you mean."

He stepped up to her and offered his arms again. Again, she leaned into him. This time her face was pressed against his chest; she lightly rested her hands on his waist. His chest was a solid wall of warmth. She could feel his heart beating; his body was full of life and strength and pressed very close to hers. Fire woke in her body. She stepped back abruptly.

"We shouldn't do that. It'll get us into trouble."

He gave her a knowing look.

"I can handle that kind of trouble."

"I bet you can."

She laughed a little, and stepped across the room to the opposite counter.

"But I can't."

"Duncan." Erin entered the room in a flurry. "You're blocking the McDaniel's. Go move your car. Please."

She tossed out the last word with a grin. Duncan smiled at Abby, his eyes alight with mischief. They were not alone for the rest of the time they were at the Gordons' home. Erin saw to that by keeping them both busy doing odd jobs. Whether she did it purposefully or not, Abby was relieved to have something constructive to do with her hands.

The two hours Abby spent at Pat's seemed like a full day's work when she was on her way home. The overcast sky let loose a weepy rain. The events of the day lay on her like wet, sodden clothes.

What was she going to do with Duncan?

He was rich and handsome, but there was something she didn't know yet. Her mom had not been forthcoming in her side of the recollection of his past. For her part, Abby could only come up with employees who thought he had stolen the family business from his brother.

And then there was Ossy Gordon who had told her to stay away from him. Ossy had died without telling her why he felt so strongly about Duncan. And whatever else he was, Ossy Gordon had been an honest man and kind to her and Chloe. She had no reason to doubt what he said.

It would be a couple of weeks before she could ask Pat anything about him out of respect for her loss. It was only her unruly heart that ran ahead without any direction that said, "Go for it," but this time she couldn't listen. She had to do what her head said and stay clear of the man that everyone warned her of even if she had fallen in love with him.

As she got close to home, she decided she would go get Chloe early from school. It would be good to have a ray of sunshine on this dismal day.

"I want to play clay!" Chloe yelled in the hallway as they walked out of the school to the car.

"It's time to go home, Chloe."

"I can't want to!" she hollered.

Chloe began to cry after they got in the car, and Abby wondered if it was such a hot idea after all. Chloe cried the whole way home, and by the time Abby pulled onto her street for the second time, Chloe was hiccupping hysterically.

She pulled into the small driveway next to a strange car. The driveway had room for just two cars, hers and her neighbor's. This car belonged to neither of them. She was too preoccupied with Chloe to worry about it much. She unbuckled the car seat for Chloe, who was too upset to do it herself.

"Come on, Chloe. Let's go in."

"No, I can't want to!" Abby reached in and picked her up. The child kicked and screamed. The blunt toes of her shoes kicked Abby's thighs.

"Hush now," she soothed, but Chloe was too worked up to stop. Abby wanted to get her inside where she could sit with her and calm her down. She walked to the back door, carrying Chloe and juggling her keys. She heard a bang on the front door when she finally made it inside.

The front doors of both apartments were encased in a small vestibule little used by either occupant. Every one of Abby's friends would have come to the back door.

Abby stepped up to the peephole. A woman of medium height with razored blonde hair stood there, holding a clipboard.

"Who is it?" Abby hollered through the door.

"Social Services." The woman's deadpan voice was gravelly, scarred-by-tobacco deep. "Will you open the door, please?"

Abby's stomach burned with fear. *Social Services? What could they want?*

Chloe was still hiccupping in the background. Abby's hand was trembling as she opened the door.

"Hello." Abby put on her best smile.

"Hi."

The woman's face didn't change. "Can I come in.?"

"Sure." Abby stepped back, and the woman entered. She was shorter than Abby and very thin. Her glasses hung on a beaded chain around her neck.

"I am Frances Gates. We've had a complaint about you."

The woman donned her glasses and scanned the room. She wrote on her clipboard.

Abby scanned the room and saw the breakfast dishes still in the sink.

"What do you mean? What kind of complaint?"

Abby picked up the sobbing Chloe.

The social worker's face softened at Chloe into an almost smile. Chloe laid her head on Abby's shoulder and looked at the woman wide-eyed.

Who would have complained about her? Who would do such a thing?

"If you cooperate, it will be better for you. Do you mind if I look around? These will explain your rights." She handed Abby a stack of leaflets.

She looked around the tiny apartment. Chloe's toys were on the floor in her room. The dishes were in the sink. There were dirty clothes in a basket in the bathroom. Her home didn't measure up. She just knew it. Even the carpet was an ugly orange. Abby started to rock Chloe.

Who would try and take her from me?

"Will you put the child down, please?"

"Why?"

"I need to see her."

"She is only three years old."

"I know that, ma'am."

Abby lowered Chloe to the floor. Her heart was sinking. She held Chloe's hand and together they walked over to the woman.

"Hi, Chloe." Frances Gate's face softened again. Like a supply clerk assessing a shipment, the smile never touched her eyes.

"Hi." Chloe held onto Abby's hand.

"Can you circle around for me, Chloe?"

"No."

"You can't?"

"Come on, Chloe sunshine." Abby raised her hand above Chloe's head in an attempt to swing her around. Chloe wouldn't cooperate.

"She's upset because I took her out of school early. She wanted to play with clay." Abby smiled at the woman. Ms. Gates gazed at her from the top of her glasses. She obviously had no time for such things.

Chloe clung to Abby's leg.

"I have seen enough today. I won't be taking Chloe with me this afternoon. You will hear from us when our investigation is complete. Here's my card. If you have any questions, you may call me."

"Good-bye, Chloe." She waved and didn't bother with the smile. "Good day to you, Ms. Ericksen."

Abby closed the door behind the woman, being careful not to slam it into her backside as she left. She went to the kitchen and sat down. She couldn't sit still. She got up and did the dishes: two cereal bowls and two spoons. It wasn't all that much, she told herself as she scrubbed them clean and put them away. Of all the days to leave them in there. Of course she could never have known that Ms. Gates was coming.

Chloe played with her toys while Abby worked out her agitation washing the clothes she should have done on the weekend. Ossy's death had drained her energy away and she hadn't felt like it.

Tears began to roll down Abby's cheeks. It was all too much for one day. Ossy's burial. Duncan... A warm sensation stole over her as she remembered the feeling she had of leaning into his arms. Duncan's mother. And now this.

How long do investigations take? Who conducts them? When will I know anything?

She looked at her daughter on the floor playing with her dolls. She was well fed. She was outgoing. Her mom always said that her outgoing personality was good. It was a gauge of her stability.

It couldn't be Brad because he'd had the chance to fight for her when they were getting the divorce. He didn't. He was in town now and hadn't been to see her. So it couldn't be him.

There was no one else. Ruth? No. She was too wrapped up in her own troubles to try causing Abby problems.

She would just have to wait until the report came. And until then she would go home.

Abby packed an overnight bag for herself and Chloe. She put it and her dulcimer in the trunk of her car, strapped Chloe into her car seat, and headed over to her mother's house.

It was a modest house, not unlike the Gordons'. She used her key to go inside and put her things in the guest room, the same room where she had spent so many summers. She had just dumped blocks on the floor to play with Chloe when she heard her mom's car in the driveway.

When she saw Helen in the doorway, she began to cry.

"What is it?" Her mom came over and sat on the floor next to her. Chloe climbed into her lap.

"Social Services came today."

"What!"

"A Ms. Frances Gates. She came and inspected my house. There's been a complaint." Abby rested her head on her mother's shoulder and sobbed. "I just wanted to come home."

"Well, you stay right here with me. Did she tell you who reported you?"

"No," Abby said and sat up straight. Chloe leaning on her while she was leaning on her mom was too much for her back.

"Well, you've got nothing to worry about. You don't have what they're looking for."

"How do you know?"

"I just do. You should see some of the kids they find. Living in filth, black and blue... You don't have any of that."

"I hope you're right. I'm just scared. Who would have done such a thing?"

"Bradley."

"But, Mom, if he wants to see her so badly, why doesn't he come and see her? Besides that, if I'm so dangerous, why did he leave her with me in the first place?"

Anger surged through her. She stood up and started to clean up the blocks by throwing them back in their box.

"That's it. If I'm so bloody awful, why did he leave her with me in the first place?"

"Good point," Helen replied.

"Too bad you don't have any connections down there at that place. You should have seen that woman. If she ever knew how to smile, it was a long time ago."

"I guess so. You don't understand what kind of stuff they see every day. It's like police work. You see a lot of the dregs of society, and it takes its toll on the good people who work there."

"Yeah, well, that's no reason to be bad to my Chloe."

"Was she bad to Chloe?" Abby could see Helen's hackles rise.

"No, not really. I am just upset."

"I'm assuming that you do not intend to move in?"

"No. I just wanted to come home for tonight. I'm so tired."

"Well, I'm gonna get changed. I've been in these scrubs all day. I've been filling in for my friend ... " Her voice trailed off as she disappeared into her room.

It was so good to be home. Chloe had dumped the blocks back out again and was building a shaky tower.

Abby remembered when the carpet in this house was a bright red floral. She had been a baby, and the house had belonged to her grandmother. Her mom had since replaced that carpet with the tasteful beige one they were sitting on.

They passed the evening pleasantly, reminiscing of the days when there were more of them. They told each other the old stories and looked forward to the day when they could share them with Chloe.

"What more have you heard of Duncan MacLeod?" Helen asked.

"Nothing really. One girl at work seems to think that he has no right to the family business. But that's none of her business, if you ask me. My friend Debbie thinks he's a hunk." She laughed at the old word. Her mom smiled.

"What do you think?"

"I like him. But that doesn't mean much. You just have to look at Brad to know that I definitely do not know how to pick men. I've been sorta waiting for you to get back to me on it. Did you find out anything?"

"No, but I did remember that it wasn't him in the ER that night. I mean he was there, but he wasn't being seen. I couldn't find out anything without the right name."

"Too bad."

"Well, maybe you should take your chances. He seems nice enough."

"What are you talking about? This whole check-him-out thing was your idea. 'Be like Aunt Mae' you said. 'Make a list.'"

Helen was smiling broadly at her. She knew something.

"All I'm saying is that you have my approval to go ahead."

"Why?"

"I heard something the other day. I can't tell you about it. But I think he's probably OK."

Abby held onto the chair she sat on. She should be elated. Duncan had shown interest in her, Lord knew how she felt about him. But now she had this investigation to get through. According to her mom, she should be all right. But she didn't know yet.

"I don't have time for that stuff right now. Maybe someday."

"You have nothing to worry about. Your apartment is clean. Chloe is not beaten. It'll be fine, although it's a good idea not to start up anything new with him until the investigation is done. You don't want them thinking that you are parading a string of uncles through Chloe's life. You know what I mean?"

"Yeah."

Helen's view of a relationship would, of course, include the modern standards of premarital sex, despite what Abby told her about the way she conducted herself. And if that's what her mother thought, then why would a complete stranger, who was not predisposed to give Abby the benefit of the doubt, think any differently?

Abby went to bed early. The stress of the last few days was telling in her mood. She was cranky. Peace and quiet were what she wanted. Time to think. *What had Helen found out*? It wasn't the first time patient confidentiality had come between Helen and a story she wanted to tell about a problem she had encountered. Abby knew her mom well enough to know that she would never find out from her the events of that night.

Well, approval or no, Abby could not have Duncan MacLeod until the investigation was finished. Her name must be cleared. Then she would be free.

She drifted into a fitful sleep and awoke unsatisfied as if she hadn't slept at all.

Chapter 29

"Duncan, it's been more than a month." The stern voice that Erin MacLeod used to discipline her boys still caused him to sit up straight and pay attention. She was sitting across the table from her son sharing coffee in the large airy kitchen of their home.

The room was nearly the size of Abby's apartment, he realized. There were large multi-paned windows across the back of the room overlooking a well-kept garden. Adjacent to it, there was a massive round table ensconced in a bank of bay windows. They sat there now blowing on hot cups of coffee.

This was what Abby must have meant. Her place was like a closet compared to this light-filled room. He had blown off her comments about her apartment. Maybe he had been in the Army too long; he didn't feel anchored to any one place as home. This was where he went home to, not where he lived.

His mother's tired smile brought his thoughts

back to the table. The lines on Erin's face were deepened with fatigue. Duncan wished he could ease her grief. He hadn't seen her really smile since before his father died.

"I know, Mom. It's just not that easy. I had forgotten all about this. It's not like I had somebody hanging around just in case I needed to get married real quick." He felt the burden of his family's legacy, like an unfinished task. "It's nothing but tradition and superstition. Like black cats and ladders, it's almost pagan."

"Is that what you think?" Amusement glittered in Erin's eyes.

"Yeah. Jesus even told the Pharisee's that they broke the law of God with their traditions."

"True." Erin's eyes gleamed. "But doesn't Isaiah say 'it is better not to vow a vow than to vow a vow—"

"And break it." They spoke in unison. Erin smiled at him.

"Duncan, you gave your word before God. This requirement does not break any of God's laws that I know of." He slumped onto the table sliding his cup forward as he did so.

"Mom."

He needed time. He wasn't sure exactly when he had chosen Abby, but it seemed he had. She was so hurt and fragile. She had run away from him the day of her interview. He did feel the Lord had spoken to him about the child. Spending time with her at the church had done the trick. He was ready.

"Get up, Duncan." He sat back up.

"I am planning Easter on the Lawn. Find someone to bring."

Erin stood to indicate the end of their interview.

And that's just how Duncan felt. He'd been interviewed and found wanting. Easter was still three weeks away. Perhaps if he was careful, and with the guidance of God, she wouldn't be frightened off.

Chapter 30

Two weeks before the grand opening, Abby was kept too busy to dwell on her troubles, including Duncan MacLeod. Every night she worked on something after Chloe had been fed, bathed, and bedded down, often falling into bed herself after midnight. She brought home pamphlets and brochures to make welcome packets for their guests at the grand opening; she worked on arrangements for the Old Thyme Festival; and she practiced her music for Easter.

On Friday night she had a rehearsal at the church. She dropped off Chloe with her mom and made her way across the little town. Abby was glad to get out and play music with her friends.

The music soothed her troubled soul. She had gone round and round in her mind, but she could not figure out who could have done such a thing to her and Chloe. Since there was no truth to Chloe being abused, someone must have misconstrued something he or she saw, or else they out and out lied. Her face flamed red with indignation when she remembered the woman at the Seven-Eleven.

It had been Wednesday evening after work and Abby stopped in to buy a bottled soda. While they were waiting in line, Chloe picked up a lollipop.

"I want lollipop."

"No," Abby had said.

The woman in front of her turned around, took the lollipop from Chloe and paid for it. She handed it back to the child with a snide look at Abby. She walked out of the store before she could hear Abby take the sucker from Chloe and tell her, "Maybe after dinner."

The condescension in the woman's eyes stayed with Abby. She saw them in the eyes of every stranger. And yet she could think of no enemy. Only Brad, but she had made their daughter available to him. He hadn't called. She hadn't seen him since the child spewed vomit across the restaurant onto his pants three weeks earlier.

Chloe was too little to understand. But one day she would. One day she would want to know why her father didn't come to see her. It was going to be hard on Chloe. But Abby was not going to chase him or teach Chloe to chase after him. If Bradley chose to fail, then he could do it without Abby making excuses or covering for him.

Duncan's truck was parked among the others when she arrived at the church. Avoiding him here would be harder, but she did have things to do. No doubt he did too or he wouldn't be here.

It would be so much easier just to talk to him and tell him what was going on, but she couldn't. Abby was embarrassed by her mother's suggestion that Chloe shouldn't appear to have a bunch of uncles. Besides that, she had to stand on her own two feet. She didn't need his power or his wealth; she would do this on her own. Then she could think about the future.

Pastor Bob was standing on the stage in the front of the sanctuary when she walked in the door. Peace came over her; she felt safe and loved here.

"Hi, Abby." Lars came in from the door that led downstairs from the back of the altar.

"Hi, guys." Abby placed her things in a pew and went up to see what she could do to help while she waited for the rest of the praise team to arrive.

"I have a praise!" Mrs. Young arrived on the altar with a giggle.

"I am glad I caught you, Abby." She laid a hand on Abby's forearm. "Lars, Pastor. Is Duncan here? I saw his truck outside."

Abby shrugged. She hadn't seen him yet.

"He's downstairs getting the brass vases for the lilies," Lars answered.

"Well, I'll just tell him when I see him. Ruth, my daughter"—she looked around to include them all—"we talked last night for the first time. I mean we really talked." Her eyes misted over at the memory. "And she called Charlie."

Abby felt the delicious tingly fingers of God. Her spirit soared.

"Hallelujah!"

"They have a date next week. I am so happy for them," Mrs. Young continued. "Who knows? Maybe someday I will get some grandchildren after all."

They all laughed.

"Well, I have a prayer request," Abby said. "A social worker came to my house on Tuesday. Someone reported me for something. I don't know

what. I'm under investigation. Please pray that they won't take Chloe from me."

Abby answered all the questions: No, she didn't know who did it; No, she didn't know what action of hers could have been misconstrued.

"And please don't tell anyone else." Talking with them and sharing her distress did nothing to alleviate the growing fear that things were going to get worse before they got better.

"Of course we won't, dear." Mrs. Young patted her arm.

"It's no one's business," breathed Lars in his sonorous voice. Pastor Bob just shook his head. His eyes spoke for him.

Abby thought it was a gift of God that it took Duncan so long to find the vases in the basement. He didn't turn up until the subject had changed to the music they were to rehearse.

The rehearsal began after Rose, the music director, arrived. It was all business after that.

Agitation over the social worker's visit was a noise in Abby's mind. She couldn't concentrate on the music. She was haunted by images of Chloe living with Brad and worse. Chloe taken into foster care. The desire to dive under a rock became severe when these thoughts presented themselves.

Abby had never had a worse practice in her life. She drove Chloe home glad it was over.

The weekend loomed before her empty, but for the waiting.

Every time she sat down to play with Chloe, Abby wondered if it would be the last time she would be able to do so with her daughter without people watching. She took that thought with her everywhere she went: the drug store, the grocery store. All eyes were surveillance cameras, watching, waiting to catch her in some evil act.

Chapter 31

Duncan drove home from church troubled. He hadn't meant to eavesdrop on Abby's prayer request. He had heard voices as he came up the back stairs. Only when he put his hand on the doorknob did he hear Abby say she had a prayer request. He waited to give her time to finish and then she said she didn't want anyone else to know. So he waited like a sneak until the subject changed. He hated deceit. Soon he would have to tell her that he had heard them. Chloe was all that Abby had or cared about. Anyone who knew her knew that. She always took seconds when it came to her kid. He'd never seen a woman wear shabbier clothes than her children. And now someone was threatening everything she had.

That was the first clue, he realized. Someone who didn't know her had to be at the heart of this. If he ever got his hands on the person who did this, he or she would be very sorry indeed. Until then, he would use his considerable resources to help her.

Of course Douggie would have to handle this.

And if he wasn't good enough, then he would find out who was. Abby would have only the best. The image of Chloe smiling up into his eyes while she ate doughnuts on the back of his truck stayed with him as he walked into the house.

Of course she wouldn't let him fight this for her. She would want to do this alone. She was independent. There was a lot to admire about Abigail Ericksen. She would fight this on her own—and fight his help.

Of course he could just marry her today and let whoever it was come after him. But she wouldn't do that either. Abby would come to him on her own terms.

She would have to come to him free and clear, or she wouldn't respect herself.

He smiled to himself; it was good that his mom would host the Easter on the Lawn.

When Duncan arrived home, he found his mother and brothers eating a late dinner in the kitchen.

"Douggie, could I see you in my office?"

He turned away from them to pour himself a glass of iced tea. *His* office. He had needed to correct himself before he spoke. He needed to think of it that way or forever stand in Lachlan's shadow. It felt good, casting off the mantle of grief. He had to choose life; Lachlan would have expected no less.

"Oooo, Duncan, is it time for the prenupts?" Andrew teased. Angus laughed.

"No. And when it is time for me to marry, there will be no prenuptial agreement. What's mine will be hers, and what is hers will be mine. Do you understand?"

Eyes all around the table were wide.   "Well, sure Duncan. We were only teasing ya."

"Now, Douglas, if you have a moment."

It was not meant to be a question. Douglas stood up and followed his brother into his study.

Duncan went in and sat down behind the desk. Then he stood up and began to clear away the desk ornaments. This was his space now, and he had work to do.

Chapter 32

Saturday morning dawned sunny and warm.
Flowers were beginning to bloom. Abby opened
every window in her apartment. A fresh wind blew
past the white bars, clearing the air. Abby felt like a
prisoner, afraid to go out because of the eyes of
others. Her strength returned as she paid her bills.

When she was done, she had money left over.
It hadn't happened since she had been divorced.
God had taken care of her. So why should she sit
behind bars hiding when He would take care of
her? She had enough money left to buy her
groceries and a new Easter outfit for Chloe.

"Come on, Chloe. We're going out."

Four hours later she returned with a trunk full
of groceries and two dress bags.

The dress she bought for Chloe was in yellow
dotted Swiss. It was smocked at the top and had
puffed sleeves. The dress she found for herself was
the same shade of yellow. It had ordinary flat
sleeves and a v-neck. She wouldn't have bought it

except it was on the clearance rack. She couldn't believe her good fortune.

It was good to get out, and it was good to be home. Her mailbox was bulging with circulars and the local weekly paper. After she put away the food, she went out front to retrieve the mail.

Wrapped in her newspaper were two letters and a bill. She tucked the bill away in the drawer reserved for that purpose and looked at the addresses on the others. The first was a card. "MacLeod" was embossed in gold on the flap. The other was a number ten business size from Social Services.

She put the others down on the counter and tore into the envelope. She had not expected to hear so soon.

"...We are closing the investigation. We have found no evidence of the claim that was made against you. We will keep your file open for one year. You may request a review if you choose. You must make this request within 30 days ... "

She was free! She broke out in a sweat. Her hands began to shake. She was free.

"Chloe!" The child came out from her room.

Abby picked her up and swung her around.

"We are free, Chloe. Free!"

"Put me down."

Abby put her down and went for the phone.

"Mom?"

"Abby?"

"Yeah. It came. They found nothing."

Her mother was entirely too calm.

"I told you you would be fine."

"I know. Aren't you excited?"

"No, I knew it would be OK. Would you like to go to dinner? My treat. I found a few Easter things for Chloe. I think you'll like them. We'll go to Sammy's."

"OK. It's sort of appropriate, isn't it? If it was Brad."

"I'll pick you up."

Abby hung up the phone and picked up the letter again. She tucked it away in her purse to share with her mother over dinner. The shining gold letters on the card caught her attention. On the back under the gold embossed lettering, which Abby thought must have cost a fortune, the letter had been sealed with an ancient crest in red wax. Abby got a butter knife from the drawer to lift the seal, so as not to crack it. The trembling of her hands exerted the right amount of pressure; the wax lifted easily off the paper. The card was the same cream color of the envelope. The writing was in script:

Mrs. Lachlan MacLeod
Requests the honor of your presence
for
Easter on the Lawn
Easter Sunday afternoon, 2:00 pm.

Her mother arrived carrying an Easter hat and gloves in a plastic bag before she had time to wonder at the invitation.

"Look at this..."

Abby handed the invitation to Helen and took the bag.

"Gramma! Gramma!" Chloe bounded into the room and ran into Helen's legs. Helen handed the invitation back to Abby unread.

"I'll look at it in a minute." She picked the child up and stuck her on a hip.

"Look what I have for you, baby girl."

"Oh, Mom, they're perfect. You always buy her the nicest things. I really appreciate it, you know."

"I thought she could use it for Easter."

"Or maybe this Easter on the Lawn thing," Abby suggested.

They rode with Helen over to Sammy's. It had been a while since Abby had been there, but now she had no reason to feel intimidated. It didn't matter if Brad showed up. She was cleared. The parking lot showed a good crowd, but wasn't too full. *It doesn't matter anyway. Let 'em look.*

Perhaps there was a window seat left.

Abby saw Duncan's gray pickup truck parked at the rear of the building as they walked into the restaurant.

Her heart soared. She could see Duncan now. There was no more need to avoid him in the hallways.

"Hey, y'all!" Sharmagne called from behind the counter. "Y'all want a window seat?"

They nodded their heads yes. Sharmagne grabbed a couple of menus and a wooden box highchair and led the way to a table for four under a plexiglass eave.

"It's seafood night."

Again Abby was facing the window. In the fading light she could see behind her in the glass. She was glad not to have to keep an unconscious lookout for Brad. She scanned the reflection for Duncan. She couldn't see him. He must be stuck on the other side of the bar. No matter, she could see him when the time was right. Now she had no need to rush. The future lay before her bright with possibilities.

Helen caught her eye by weaving her body back and forth.

"I don't think he'll be back here."

"I wasn't looking for Bradley."

Abby leaned toward her mother over the table. "I think I saw Duncan's truck when we came in."

Helen's eyes filled with glee.

"Do you see him here?"

"No, he must be on the other side of the bar."

Helen began searching, her eyes darting here and there. The years dropped from her face when she was playful, and Abby was thankful at that moment for everything. Her eyes filled with tears. She squeezed them closed long enough to clear the liquid.

"Well, I'm gonna go to the bar. I'll be right back."

"OK, honey."

Abby chose a pre-warmed plate from the stack sitting on the side of the counter that held the hot food items. She kept her eyes down at first. If he was indeed on this side of the bar she didn't want him to think she was spying on him. A spoonful of mashed potatoes and a couple of fried clams later, she dared to look up through the sneeze shield. Across the room he sat with a heaping plate, laughing with Ruth Abercrombie.

Chapter 33

Ice-hot humiliation speared through Abby cutting off her rosy visions of the future.

Of course. Ruth. She was more in his league. Flashy, self-confident. Certainly capable of meeting physical needs that Abby was not prepared to deal with until after she was married.

It had been foolish of her to think of Duncan MacLeod, the most eligible bachelor in town. He wouldn't be interested in an employee—an employee with a child, no less.

She gathered some more odds and ends for Chloe to nibble on and retreated to her table.

"Did you see him?" Helen's eyes were full of mischief.

"Yes. He has a date."

"You probably misunderstood. Why would Duncan MacLeod, the richest guy in town, bring a date here? I mean, it's nice and all... " Helen's eyes still reflected playful mischief.

Abby felt no hope.

"I don't know. It isn't any of my business," Abby said. "I'll be right back."

This time, as she filled a plate for herself, she could not force herself to stop looking at the couple. They were sitting at a table next to a window. The blinds were drawn. Duncan's bit of plaid hung out of his jacket pocket. Ruth looked more like the porcelain doll Abby had always associated with Ruth. They did not see her. They were too absorbed in conversation and laughter to notice her staring. She walked away when Duncan reached over and placed his hand on Ruth's folded arm.

"I think I have to stop coming here," she told Helen when she returned with a scanty plate of food.

"Things are not always what they seem," her mother reminded her. Then she got up to retrieve dinner for herself.

"Well, at least you don't have to worry about Social Services anymore," Helen said as she scooted back into her chair. The mirth was gone from her eyes.

"I told you."

"Like I said. Things are not always what they seem, Abby."

"I know that, Mom. But this is pretty clear. Maybe that's what this invitation is all about." She laid the creamy envelope on the table.

"Nah," Abby recanted, "it's too soon for all that."

"What do you mean?" Helen asked.

"She's still married." *Poor Charlie*, Abby thought, *no one could compete with Duncan MacLeod.*

"Well, that makes things difficult."

"Let's not talk about them anymore. Where did you go today?"

They spent the rest of their dinner pleasantly engaged in talking about shopping and other safe subjects.

Lying in bed that night, Abby buried her hopes of Duncan MacLeod. She convinced herself that she had misread everything he had ever said. Surely all he ever meant to be was her friend. She was miserable, but she knew she would get over it. She would have to. Life goes on.

She was cleared of any wrongdoing as far as Chloe went, and she had a good job, despite the dodging she would have to do to avoid Duncan. The Lord was still on His throne. All in all, things were looking up.

Monday morning she was sitting at her desk reminding herself that things were looking up, when a patch of plaid, framed by Duncan MacLeod, stood in front of her.

"Hello," he said.

Abby's breath still caught when she looked into his brown eyes. It would go away in time, she reminded herself.

"Hi."

"Care to walk with me?"

"Well"—she waved over her desktop that was filled with invitations and other paperwork—"I am a little busy."

"Exactly. I'd like an update." He turned on his heel and headed out. Abby followed close behind.

"I have meetings all day, so we'll talk while we walk."

Duncan listened as she told him the preparations she had made. She had followed his instructions impeccably: the caterer, the people she'd invited, the responses. Out of the hundreds of invitations, seventy percent had responded affirmatively. It would be a large crowd. Good.

"Listen, for the entertainment, I don't know if Andrew has talked with you yet, but I asked him to sing and play. It's an old family tradition."

"I was hoping we could get him to play the pipes." She dazzled him with her smile.

Now came the hard part. They were standing by his truck in the parking lot. He had given himself plenty of time for this talk. He had meetings, but they didn't begin for another hour.

"On a different subject," he began. Abby looked him in the eye, the jade of her eyes luminescent.

"I have to tell you—the other night, at choir practice, I was on the stairs. I heard you tell the others about the Social Services investigation."

She crossed her arms over her chest.

"I am sorry. I did not intentionally listen in. It was just one of those things—I had hold of the doorknob—I should have just come in. I'm sorry."

She was not making this any easier for him, standing there with her arms folded. He couldn't read her. The jade had turned to stone.

"The reason I'm telling you now is because I want to offer you my help. If I can do anything—"

"It's over." Abby didn't move. "I was cleared."

"You must be relieved."

"I am."

"Well, I guess you won't need my help then."
He looked at the ground.

"No, I won't."

"If it turns out that you do—you know, for
something else—my brother is a lawyer. And if you
need any help, all you have to do is tell me."

He'd never felt so awkward in all his life.

"Thanks, I'll keep that in mind. Now if there
isn't anything else, I'll get back to work."

"Sure thing."

She walked away from him, slowly, head high.
When she went into the building, he turned and got
in his truck. He would give anything to know what
she was thinking. *Why had she not told him about
the investigation?* he wondered for the thousandth
time. He knew that she wasn't going to accept his
help, but at least now she knew that he was there to
help if the situation got worse. And it was going to
get much worse if what Ruth had told him was the
truth, and he was willing to bet it was. He started
the ignition. Now he had forty-five minutes to kill
before his meetings at the fishery.

Chapter 34

Abby couldn't think. She walked deliberately back into the building and took her seat at her desk. Her brain was in a fuzz. She wished that it didn't happen every time she was caught off guard.

Duncan knew about Social Services. No wonder he dumped her for Ruth Abercrombie. Of course, he didn't know what kind of life Ruth had been leading. Was he another one of her conquests? Well, even if he was, it was none of her business. She wouldn't tell anyone what Ruth had confessed to her in private.

Besides which, she had no right to be jealous anyway. He was not hers, and never would be. She just needed to get over it and move on. Perhaps she should consider looking for a new job. This one was great for perks, but the atmosphere was becoming treacherous. She surveyed the cluttered piles on her desk.

Well, she wasn't going anywhere for a while, not with a grand opening on Friday. And the band letters had started to come back for the Old Thyme

Festival. It was going to be a busy summer—much too busy to be worrying over Duncan MacLeod.

Chapter 35

"Douglas, is that you?" Erin called from the doorway of the spacious kitchen.

"Yes, Mother," he answered. Douglas's speech had gotten formal during law school. Erin found the stiffness irritating. *Mother* indeed.

"Come in here, will you?"

Douglas entered the room before Erin could rejoin Andrew at the round table set in the bay windows. She loved sitting there in her garden without the muss of dirt under her feet and mosquitoes buzzing around her ankles and elbows.

She saw the boys exchange questioning looks.

"Sit down, Douglas. I want to talk to you and your brothers."

"Jeez, Ma—lighten up," Andrew said grinning at Douglas, who sat down.

"Hush. I will speak to Angus later." Again the two exchanged glances. Erin had a brief stab of pleasure. She had her boys with her. Poor Pat. Her children had gone off. Both of them lived away from home. Now her husband was in the ground. They shared that. The brilliance had gone out of Erin's life; it lay buried with Lachlan. But her sons were home, even restless, wild Duncan. He was her concern now.

"We need to talk about Duncan."

"Are ya' taking to gossip, now, Ma? I for one would love to know what has crawled up his—" He cut himself short.

"Andrew."

"All I meant is he's been surly. Damn hard to get along with."

"Let Mother speak, Andrew." The gavel dropped in Douglas's voice.

"Hush, both of you." Erin paused. "What have you found out about Abigail Ericksen?"

Douglas's face went blank.

"How do you know about that?"

"Never mind about that." She knew her middle son, a skeptic from birth, made worse with education, was always looking into the backgrounds of the people and businesses with whom the MacLeod's came in serious contact. Of course he'd been looking into the background of Abigail Ericksen. She was not going to explain why she knew that Abigail was important to Duncan. There were some things a mother didn't need to explain.

Douglas considered for a moment and then said, "It won't do any harm to tell you that she is exactly who she says she is."

"Whoa—that's deep," Andrew quipped.

"Good. That's all we need for the present."

"Andrew, what song have you chosen for the grand opening?" Erin said.

"It's a sea song. About a young girl whose man goes off to sea. While he's gone she weds another. When the seafaring man comes back he wants his girl. She goes with him. Once they've gone out to sea she becomes lonesome for the first man she married. Then the boat sinks, and they all die."

"Perhaps you should choose something less tragic," Erin suggested.

"Yes, Andrew. We don't want people getting the idea boats aren't safe," Douglas said.

"Lighten up, Doug. It's just an old folk song," Andrew said.

"Andrew, perhaps you should sing one of our songs. The wedding song," Erin suggested.

"But we don't just sing that one anywhere, do we? I thought it was just for weddings."

"Not always. It's one of our stories, and I think it's a good time to hear some of the old songs. It would please your father, Andrew, and me as well."

"If you feel that strongly about it, Ma, I'll do it for ya'. Duncan's givin' me a free hand. I can sing what I like."

"Thank you, Andrew." She reached across the table and put her hand over his. He grinned.

Chapter 36

Friday morning, streamers were hung from the light poles to the stone building. Boys from the caterer arrived and began unloading tables from a white box van. A couple of crewmen unfolded the first of two large blue-and-white striped tents. Abby could feel the energy of the excited people. It was going to be a big bash. The town of Ocean View had few notable events, and this year, this would be one of them. A reporter from the local weekly roamed around taking pictures. Later they would have a brief program rehearsal.

The program would be short, consisting mostly of a speech by Duncan, and Andrew would sing. It would give the whole presentation a good Scottish flavor.

The caterer was the oldest and best in Ocean View. The guests from near and far were in for a treat.

Two large tents were erected: one for receiving guests, and one for the large reception. The grills were warming up at the back of the catering tent.

The smell of barbecue rode on the breeze.

Kay trudged by Abby carrying one of three large boxes of information packets. Debbie came by lugging another. They would be helping in reception. Abby followed.

"Didn't you say you had three of these boxes?" Kay asked.

"Yes. Didn't you see them in the office?"

"No. Just these two," Debbie said.

"Are you sure?"

"Yep," Kay tossed out as she headed back toward the building. Abby followed. She was sure she had brought all the brochures from home. She had taken all the packet materials home and worked on them there. It was so much easier to spread everything out on the floor and fill the envelopes that way. Once she had completed them, she alphabetized them and filled three boxes. Then she had hauled the three boxes to her trunk one at a time.

Abby searched her office and the outer office. She popped her head into Angus's space and even Andrew's. Nothing. She must have left them at home. She had no choice but to go get them. She told Debbie where she was going and hopped into her car. They could not do without the packets. She had packed ones for each company and one extra for those who might show up unexpectedly. The box containing those for their clients was missing.

From the street, she could see a newspaper-type advertisement hanging out of the mailbox. She parked in her allotted space and got out. She hurried to the mailbox to retrieve the junk mail feeling a little guilty for doing her own personal business on company time. She stopped short when she saw an envelope tacked to her front door.

The tack popped off the door easily. In she went.

There it was—the box. Somehow she had managed to leave it right there by the door.

Abby put her keys and junk mail on the counter and opened the envelope that had been stabbed to her door. The paper cut her thumb as she peeled the flap open. She stuck her thumb in her mouth and fumbled the letter out of its envelope. It was a subpoena. She was to be in court in two weeks. Bradley Ericksen was suing for custody of Chloe.

Abby felt a cool wave pass through her neck and drift down her spine. She folded the papers and put them in her pocket. She hefted the box and put it on the backseat of her car. She went back in after her keys, locked the door, and drove back to work. She would have to get an attorney. She would ask her mother to recommend someone. She could ask Pat. Duncan had told her that his brother was a lawyer. She wondered just how many brothers he had. Anyway, she couldn't ask him to help her. He had his own troubles, and she had vowed to stay away from him. He had done enough for her and Chloe. He had given her a good job, and the least she could do for him was repay his kindness with freedom. No, she would do this herself.

When she arrived at the dock, the festivities were beginning. The tents were up, a piper was playing, and the smell of barbecue permeated the breeze. Every employee of MacLeod was dressed in a yellow kilt. It had the look of a county fair.

A small clutch of well-dressed people stood around the reception tent. Abby hauled the box out of the backseat of her car and brought it over to the tables just in time. She smoothed out her yellow kilt that she had thought to take no care of until that moment. She was glad she hadn't torn it or smeared it hauling that box around. Her fingers flew to her grandfather's tie pin clasped under the collar of her plain white blouse. It was still there. The subpoena lay folded in her pocket.

These were the first of the arrivals. Her guests. She stuck out her hand and introduced herself. White teeth, tanned faces, unnaturally thin, the waifs of the travel industry passed by with the usual banalities. It seemed to Abby that she had a tape recording in her head for this sort of thing. She took it out and played it at the appropriate times. Things like, "So nice of you to come" and "If you need anything let me know" came forth from the smile on her face as if she meant them. The folded paper in her pocket reminded her of the battle that lay ahead.

The parking lot and the dock area were filling fast. Their guests came in clumps moving like jellyfish in the surf, ebbing and flowing with the tides, dipping below the surface to reemerge a few feet away from where they had been.

Internal radar told her that Duncan had arrived. She could see him moving through the corridors made by the backs of the clusters, becoming one of them for a time, extracting himself, and then joining another. He was smiling broadly, gesturing towards the yacht that lay waiting at the dock.

He had everything under control. He walked smoothly among the bunches of guests. She was proud of him. She wished she could share all her troubles with him. Surely those shoulders were strong enough for this fight.

You've gotta stop thinking like that, she told herself. *You can rely on God. He will help you out of this.*

A tap on the shoulder caused her to jump. She turned to find Pat.

"Didn't mean to scare you, Abby. You seemed a long way off."

"You're right. I was a long way off. So what brings you out here? Want to take a cruise?" They laughed together.

"I came with Erin MacLeod. She thought it would be good to get me out. She was right." She looked around at the crowds. "You know, after a funeral, the oddest thing happens. All the people go home. Of course they have to. Martha had to take her boys home—they're in school, you know."

"I didn't think of that. How quiet it must be."

"It is. The day after Martha left, the doorbell rang. It was Erin. She knew. So here I am. Out and about. Have you seen Duncan?"

"Yes. He's over there." Abby pointed toward the *Erin~D*. Duncan stood in front of a small cluster of people, obviously answering questions and inviting people to tour the vessel. Angus stood at the stern ready to receive any who came aboard. She could just see Kay standing behind him peeking out of the cabin.

"He looks fine today," Pat said.

Abby felt a blush rise to her cheeks.

"So you did notice. Have you seen anything of him?" Pat asked.

"No, not really. I think he's interested in someone else." Abby avoided Pat's eyes by keeping her gaze out at the festivities she was supposed to be watching.

"Are you quite sure about that, Abby?"

"Yes. Will you excuse me? I see that they are turning on the mike, and I have to get up to the stage. I'm on!" She smiled at Pat and made a speedy escape. Abby felt a twinge of guilt at rushing off, but it wasn't a lie. She did need to get to the stage. The squeal of the microphone had saved her.

Abby stood around on her tiptoes for five minutes backstage watching for Duncan and Andrew.

"Hello, beautiful." Andrew arrived first carrying bagpipes and a guitar.

"Hi. Have you seen your brother?" Abby asked.

"I'm here," Duncan said.

His brown eyes were flat and guarded. The last time she had seen him, she hadn't exactly been friendly. Was he angry?

When Abby stepped across the stage, the piper stopped. She picked up the microphone.

"Hello, everyone!" People turned to face the stage slowly. "Welcome."

When she had the attention of most of them, she introduced Duncan. He stepped up to the mike, and she stepped back off the stage. He would take it from here. It was his show. She found herself a metal folding chair stuck by a wooden crate near a tent stake and sat down. She listened to his voice. It had a lilt, soft and barely discernable. She felt it calling to her soul, tugging and pulling. Abby placed her hand over the pocket with the thick folded paper.

No.

Duncan briefly explained his vision for the

Erin~D. He told how he and his father had dreamed up the scheme and the hours of phone calls and e-mails it had taken to make their dream a reality. He invited any who wished to climb aboard and experience her accommodations. Then he introduced Andrew, one of his four brothers.

Well, that answers that, she thought wryly; there were four brothers.

"I have an ancient song to play for ye." The lilt in Andrew's voice was more an impersonation than the real thing.

"'Tis a good day for old songs... " He plucked and tuned his guitar. "This one was a favorite of Lachlan MacLeod's. Today I sing it for my mother."

"Shall I tell you a tale of the first Duncan MacLeod?" Andrew began to sing and strum. Abby perked up. She loved old ballads.

"He decided to seek, his fortune abroad
a new land to conquer, begin a new life.
He thought to take no one—not even a wife.

On the day of his leavin' fair Fiona McBride
She walked right up to him and made a
small bow.
It's high time I speak to thee my Duncan
MacLeod.
I vow to go with ye, I care not how.

She gave him a cloth that her mother had
made, it was
made of fine linen, it was all that she owned.
He took the gift from her and then he did say
My life will be hardship and ne'r will be gay.

I shall share in your hardship, your trouble,
your pain.
I shall bear you fine children to carry your
name.
Only leave me not behind thee, dear Duncan
MacLeod.
I vow to go with thee I care not how.
So he took the fair Fiona to be his bride.

She bore him five fine children that carry his
name,"

Abby's foot tapped with the beat. The song reminded her of "Sweet Betsy from Pike." It was the last verse that stuck in her mind.

"The legend holds true of the Lairds of
MacLeod.
Today they'll not marry 'til she makes a bow.
Approach him quite slowly and offer your
prize
"Tis the only way to become our Laird's fair
bride."

Andrew finished with a flourish. Abby clapped enthusiastically. *What a wonderful song*, she thought. *I wonder if he'll teach it to me.* As he began to play the pipes, she got up and wandered away humming the tune of "Duncan MacLeod." She thought to get a bite of barbecue. She had not eaten since breakfast, and her stomach was beginning to complain.

Chapter 37

"Doesn't he have a lovely voice?" It was Pat. She was dabbing a little barbecue onto a plastic plate.

"It was an interesting song. I should ask him to teach it to me. Do you think he will?" Abby asked. She began to fill a plate for herself.

"I don't know. I think it's one of their family songs, isn't it?"

"He said that, but I thought he was kidding. He probably wrote it himself."

"I don't know. A lot of the old songs are passed down this way. Sung at festivals of importance. But that's not what I want to talk to you about, Abby. Before Ossy died, he resolved an old problem, and I think you need to be told about it. I think he wanted me to tell you."

Pat looked like she was going to cry, so Abby took her by the arm with her free hand and led her to the far corner of the dock where nothing of interest lay for the throngs.

They sat down on the weathered boards and hung their feet over the edge. Abby worried a little about losing one of her pumps so she kept angling her feet up from the ankles. And though she felt odd trying to keep her shoes on, she thought Pat looked even more out of place. It was like seeing the first lady or some other dignitary sitting on the ground in fine clothes.

"It's a little quieter over here anyway."

Pat nodded in agreement. Abby waited until Pat was ready, glad to be away from the bustle of the opening and the hostile eyes of Duncan MacLeod.

"When Max was a little boy his best friend was Duncan MacLeod." Pat kept her eyes on the Bay as if the past played on the waves and she could read its cipher.

"The two of them—you should have seen 'em—they were wild. They did everything together...Boy Scouts...everything. Ossy encouraged it. He and Lachlan, that's Duncan's father, were friends, so it seemed natural. One night—oh, gosh, you should have seen them getting ready for the pinewood derby. They sanded those little cars and painted them right on our steps. Duncan spilled bright red paint on the step. It's still there. You should have seen him—white faced—telling Ossy what he'd done. He was a good boy. But they got wild as they got older." Pat continued to look out to sea.

Abby followed her gaze and waited. Andrew was playing a jig on the bagpipes now. She could almost see men and women in old Scottish garb dancing on their toes. It made her want to River Dance.

"One night," Pat started, "the boys were out

bashing mailboxes—"

Abby let out a giggle. How many boys had she known who had done that in high school? She had never done it herself; she was a good girl. But she had heard all the stories. It was a pastime that nearly qualified as a sport in the county. All that was needed was a driver and a baseball bat. Nowadays, the only thing she could think of was how much the mailboxes would cost to replace.

"It wasn't funny that night. Max was driving; Duncan was hitting the boxes. Then they came to Hermit Hogan's place. He had heard them coming up the road, and he got ready. The result was that Max was shot. He lost the use of his left arm for life. Anyway, Duncan drove him to the hospital and called us. Then he left. Lachlan felt that the boy was out of his control, so he signed the necessary papers and put him in the Army. Duncan shipped out without ever coming to see Ossy."

"So that's what it was about—Ossy telling me to stay away from Duncan."

"Yes. The day after Ossy came home from the emergency room, Duncan came to see him. He looked just like that little boy so long ago. Just as white-faced as he was then. He asked for forgiveness." Pat's eyes filled with tears. One escaped and ran down her cheek. "Os forgave him, of course. He was only angry that Duncan had never come. He ran away. He asked Duncan to take care of my affairs. I've never had a head for money matters. Figures always eluded me."

Abby took her hand. "It's gonna be OK, Pat."

"I know it is. He's never let me down yet." Pat pointed a finger to the sky.

The two women hugged before Abby stood up

to go. She had finished her lunch and needed to get back to work.

"Thank you," Abby said.

"People change, Abby—Jesus changes them. Don't let pride get in the way of anything He is trying to do for you." Abby nodded and walked back toward the throngs of people.

She was glad for Duncan that he had straightened out the past with Ossy. And she supposed that was the night that her mother attended Max Gordon, which was why she couldn't find out what had happened that night.

So, her mother said that Duncan was OK. Pat said Duncan was OK. But she had seen him with Ruth, and she had a thickly folded notice in her pocket that told her Duncan was not OK. All bets were off. God would just have to send someone else. Duncan couldn't be the one.

The sun was setting as the last car pulled out of the parking lot.

Abby knew that Duncan stood behind her. Her spirit seemed to reach out from her heart through her back and bump into him. She waited before turning around, breathing deeply and bracing herself for the way she felt when she saw him. As she turned, the world went quiet. She was aware of her co-workers under the tents packing up boxes; of the caterers cleaning the grills and taking them down; the MacLeod men removing streamers, breaking down the stage, wrapping up cords. Duncan stood before her in a white shirt and kilt. His face spoke of concern. His eyes were soft brown again.

He's the one. She heard the voice of the Lord as clearly as she could hear the laughter of the workmen.

"Are you OK?"

Duncan stepped forward to put his hands on her shoulders. Abby heard "OK."

"I'm fine. Thank you."

She had no time to react to this new revelation other than to release the joy that sprang from her soul. She smiled at him. He stepped back quickly.

Oh yeah—Ruth, she remembered. Of course he must be careful with her on account of Ruth.

Well, maybe she was mistaken. Perhaps it was just her rebellious heart speaking to her after all and not the Lord.

"You seem a little dazed. Are you sure you're all right?" Abby heard him ask. She still felt a little detached.

"Yes, I'm fine. I'm sorry. I was a little lost in thought." She laughed. "Maybe a lot lost in thought."

"I thought everything went wonderfully today. You did a tremendous job. Just tremendous." His eyes sparkled.

"Thank you." She bowed a little.

"I'd like to take you to dinner to celebrate. We can pick up Chloe and go," he said.

"Chloe is spending the night with my mom."

His eyes shot up.

"Well, I wasn't sure how long this thing would go on, you know."

"Of course. Whatdya think? We can drop off your car at your house and go from there."

"Why not?"

And why not? she asked herself as she drove

home. If the Lord really did speak to her didn't she have the right—even the obligation—to check it out?

Duncan followed behind her in his gray pickup. What should she wear? Hangers of clothes slid by in her mind. She should take a shower. She felt grimy from being out at the dock all day. Would he mind waiting? Never mind. It was too much trouble, and besides she didn't want to appear overeager. A couple of friends going out to dinner. That's all. And besides, if the Lord had spoken, then Duncan would have to take her as she was. Not dressed up. Just her—problems and all.

It seemed to be fine with him because when she pulled into her driveway, he sat and waited in the truck with the engine running. Abby was glad she had thought better of a new outfit.

The corner of the envelope poked her thigh and deflated her pleasurable feelings of excitement as she slid in beside Duncan. She felt an urge to grasp her daughter in her arms. This could be one of the last nights she could spend with Chloe. She had no business going out to dinner with Duncan. She could be putting Chloe to bed. She should be consulting her mother about what to do. She had had no time all day to think of it. What was she going to do about Bradley? Perhaps she would ask Duncan about his brother, the attorney.

Duncan smiled at her once she had closed the door and settled under her seat belt.

"I thought we would go to Limon's."

"Oh, I've never been there."

"It's my favorite seafood place."

"Sounds good to me."

Duncan watched the road. Abby watched the

trees go by, their new green leaves glowing neon in the periwinkle dusk. As they drove on the winding road out of town, they passed cow pastures. Abby kept her eyes out for the first signs of lightning bugs. They made the nighttime woods around her home enchanted in the summer.

They parked in a sandy lot and walked a short, twisted road to the famed Limon's. It was more upscale than Abby was used to. She hoped it wouldn't require vast knowledge of forks. It wasn't until they reached the door that she realized they were still wearing matching clothes.

"Oh, my gosh, we are dressed like twins." She turned and nearly knocked him off the step behind her. He reached out and grabbed her waist to steady himself, and guide her forward.

"I like it."

Abby flamed red and turned around. He held the door with an arm above her head and she stepped through the doorway.

The room was golden and warm. They were standing in a long foyer carpeted in presidential blue. The walls were cream, and the accents were gold. Behind an oaken lectern stood a tall blonde man in a black tuxedo.

"Good evening, Mr. MacLeod. If you'll follow me."

Outclassed. No doubt about it, was all Abby could think as she followed the maître d' as he glided through the maze of round tables with starched white tablecloths. At the back of the room was a large wall with windows cut of small panes. From the floor to the ceiling, the windows provided a view of the Chesapeake Bay. It was toward one of these window tables that he led them.

It was quieter here than home alone at night with Chloe in bed. She was glad that her murmur of thanks was swallowed up in the plush room, as she had feared it would echo around the huge cavern and stun the other diners.

The other diners were much older than she or Duncan, yet many of them nodded and smiled at him. Then they returned to their hushed conversations. Abby was glad to see only two forks. She could handle that.

"You OK?"

Duncan was laughing at her. The twinkle in his eye warmed her.

"Yes."

"You looked a little doe-eyed there for a minute."

"It's a very nice place." She looked around again at all the finery in the room. Dark blue drapes hung at the windows were tied back with golden tassels.

"The food's good."

"Andrew was great today."

"Yep, he was. I was surprised at his choice of songs, though."

"What do you mean?" They were interrupted by a waiter with menus and a wine list. Duncan ordered stuffed flounder and a glass of white wine for each of them.

"So tell me: how is Chloe? I know how relieved you are that the Social Services thing is over."

"I am. I haven't yet figured out who turned me in."

He's the one, echoed in her thoughts.

"So what surprised you about Andrew's songs?" Abby hoped to change the subject before she spilled her guts about the letter that lay in her pocket.

"It was the choice of songs. The Scots always have music at a gathering. It just isn't a party without it. And there are certain songs that go with certain gatherings. The first one he sang was a wedding song. I thought it was funny that he chose it."

"I was going to ask him to teach it to me. Is it true?"

"Is what true?" He wasn't going to make this easy. He hadn't brought her out to get a proposal. He was interested in Chloe. And Bradley Ericksen was up to no good. He was sure of it. He would probably try to take the child. And he wasn't going to let him.

"About the laird of MacLeod. Does the girl have to ask him to marry?"

"Yes." Duncan felt his face getting red as Abby giggled.

"So that means you—right? You have to wait until some woman asks you."

"Yes, but not just any woman..."

"I think you're in for a long wait. Our society is liberal, but it's not that free."

"True, but it's happened before," Duncan reminded her.

"Your parents, you mean."

"And theirs," he said.

"What happens if no one asks you?"

"I lose all my fortune, and I will be buried in

unconsecrated ground."

"That sounds serious," she said, her eyes bright with mirth.

"Oh, it is. It has to do with vowing a vow before the Lord."

Duncan told her the story of his beatnik mother on bended knee. And about his great-grandfather who lost it all by breaking the rules.

He felt close to her then, telling her of himself. He wanted to hear more about her. He knew he needed to warn her about Bradley and Suzie. But that could come later, after they had taken a break and had a good time. She told him stories of her life: where Chloe was born and a little more than he needed to know about her birth. But that didn't stop him from wishing that he had been there, that Chloe was his—his child with her eyes.

They both refused dessert but ordered coffee.

"I need to tell you something," Duncan began.

The slight change in his tone caught Abby's attention.

"What is it?" she answered looking directly into his eyes.

"I had dinner with Ruth Abercrombie..."

"Yes, I know."

She's jealous. The thought slapped him like a wet towel.

"It's not what you think."

"I don't think anything. You can go out with whoever you want."

Her jealousy pleased him.

"I asked her out to find out about her and to see if she was a threat to you. My brother said that the people you know could be a threat to the investigation with Social Services. So I went to her to find out what was wrong with her so that she couldn't hurt you."

Abby's eyes widened. Had Ruth told him about her addiction and what it had driven her to do?

"Did she tell you?"

"Yes. I thought she was into gambling or something like that. You know you just can't take any chances."

"Well, I haven't seen her in a while."

"I asked her to stay away."

"What?"

"Don't be angry. We have to do whatever is necessary to protect Chloe. I think Bradley is going to try and take her from you. He may kidnap her. Have you thought of that?"

"Not seriously."

"It happens, Abby."

"I know. But that's not what he's going to do." She reached under the table, pulled out a thick white envelope, and put in on the table in front of him.

The waiter refilled their cups while Duncan read the documents.

"It's a subpoena."

"I know. He wants to take Chloe."

"When did you get this?"

"Today." She told him about going home to get the missing box of envelopes.

"Will you let me help?"

"Why?" Duncan reached across the table and took her hand.

"Because I love you and I love Chloe, and she deserves to stay where she is happy and grow up with the wonderful mother God gave her."

Abby hesitated, expecting her thoughts to scramble. He said he loved her. Could it be true? Her pride screamed *No*, her heart desperately gasped *Yes*. She heard the cool voice of Pat Gordon. 'Don't let pride get in the way of anything He is trying to do for you.'

"Yes." Her voice was a whisper. She shook her head firmly trying to silence any contrary thoughts.

"You know what is really odd?" Abby finally said. "He didn't want her. He's been in town for a month and has only seen her a couple of times. You'd think if he wanted her that badly he would have come to see her."

"I meant what I said, Abby. I love you."

"I heard you. I just can't think about it right now."

"I think we can settle this thing out of court."

"Why?"

"Because everything he's done is stacked against him. He left, didn't visit, or show any desire to see Chloe until now. And as you said, he hasn't even done that much since coming to town. I don't think he can win."

Abby felt enormous relief. She struggled to keep her eyes open on the way home. They passed by fields, and Abby imagined the lightning bugs flitting in and out of an enchanted forest.

"Sleepy?"

"No. It's been a long day. I think I'm relieved. I've been in knots over this thing for weeks. It's my worst nightmare come to life."

"It'll be OK."

"I hope so."

"It will be. He's never let me down yet."

They sat in the truck in Abby's driveway. Duncan held her hand. Abby's heart was glowing. Duncan separated their hands and put his arm around her. She just fit in the crook of his shoulder. He smelled wonderful. In an instant, the electric current between them crackled and zapped away the drowsy atmosphere in the small space.

She looked up at him and back down at her hands.

"What did you mean...you love me?" He tipped her chin toward him and brushed her lips with a brief kiss. When she didn't move, he deepened the kiss, his lips soft, full of tenderness over hers.

"Does that answer your question?"

Abby sat up straight.

"I had better go in."

Duncan pulled away and put his hands on the steering wheel.

"Good night," she said.

"The tartan suits you, Abby."

Chapter 38

Abby had not been able to shake the desperate need to see Chloe, so she changed into her blue jeans and a sweat shirt, packed some clothes for the morning, and drove to her mother's house.

It wasn't late, and Abby found her mother as she knew she would, sitting in front of an old movie on television working on her latest needlework.

"What are you doing here? I didn't expect to see you until noon tomorrow."

Abby didn't answer the little jab at her sleeping habits.

"I came to see Chloe." She brushed past Helen and headed down the hall to her baby. Chloe lay there, one leg crooked out on top of the blankets. Abby tucked her leg back in and kissed her child on the forehead. Her heart ached, and her back hardened. She knew that she could do whatever it took to keep Chloe with her.

Her mother had resumed her sewing by the time Abby emerged from the bedroom, but she had turned off the television.

"You want some coffee?" Helen asked without looking up.

"No, thanks. I just came from dinner."

"Why did you come here?"

"I got a subpoena today."

Helen put down her needle.

"For what?"

"Brad is suing for custody."

"Let me see it." Helen stuck out her hand for the documents. For the first time, Abby wondered if she had done the right thing in giving the document to Duncan. It was so hard to think clearly, with no mistakes. And she couldn't afford any.

"I gave it to Duncan. His brother is an attorney. I'm going to let him help me with this."

"Don't worry about the money. I'll help you."

"I hadn't gotten that far yet," Abby replied. She lay back on the couch, hands over her face.

"Well, what did the subpoena say?"

"Nothing much. Just to be in court on Thursday in two weeks."

"That's fast."

"I thought so too. Duncan is going to talk to his brother, and he'll call me."

Helen stood up.

"Well, I'm gonna get some coffee."

Abby followed her to the kitchen.

"I thought you were trying to avoid Duncan MacLeod. I thought today was the big grand opening. How did you manage to see him long enough to give him the papers?"

"It was—he took me to dinner afterward. Get this: Duncan is the head of his family, right? Today I heard an old family song, and it turns out that in order to be married, the head of their family has to be asked by the woman he weds."

Helen's eyebrows shot up, and a look of mischief returned to her eyes.

"I could do it," she said. Abby knew it was true; Helen could do it.

"I don't know if I could." Abby wrapped her arms around herself.

"Sure you could—if you wanted it bad enough."

"What would you do if he said no?" Abby asked.

"I'd be a little embarrassed, but I'd walk away with my head up. It's no different than a man asking a woman. I've often thought of that. I'm glad I'm a woman." Helen paused; the coffee was ready. She poured two cups and grabbed a box of cake doughnuts. When they sat down, she resumed. "Can you imagine the courage it takes when you're, say, thirteen, you see a beautiful girl, the prettiest one in the class or maybe not. Maybe you just think she's pretty, but you have to ask her to dance. You'd be scared to death."

"I always think of the wallflower girl, like me. Waiting to be asked, sitting in a chair, hopeful."

"Exactly. Think of all those boys. It must be murder." She took a doughnut and broke it in half.

"Must be," Abby agreed. "Duncan told me he loves me."

"That's nice. What about Ruth whatsername?" The words were as soaked in sarcasm as the coffee-sodden doughnut that had just left the coffee for her mouth.

"It was about me, he said. Ruth is into some pretty rough stuff—stuff I can't talk about. He told her to stay away from me. He seems to think that I need to be careful of who I associate with in order to protect Chloe." She told Helen about Duncan overhearing her on the steps at church. "He seemed to know that Brad was going to come after Chloe."

"Well, if you want him, you know what you'll have to do."

"I know, but it will have to wait. Chloe comes first."

Abby was feeling peaceful on all fronts but one. She had finished the grand opening; the plans for the Old Thyme Festival were coming along just fine; the *Erin~D* was ready for cruising and awaited only her guests. This one last battle was keeping the pace in her bloodstream up. Brad could not have Chloe and that was that. She didn't know how it would happen, but she would not let him have her. Even the peaceful remembrances of this house could not calm the agitation she felt every time she thought of it.

The ring of the phone jolted them both out of their chairs. It was Duncan calling to tell her Douglas had agreed to meet with her tomorrow.

"So fast?"

"No time to waste. I don't want to lose Chloe."

After coffee, after talking with her mom, it was those words that she took to bed with her. He didn't want to lose Chloe.

Chapter 39

"She's a wimp."

"I don't know, Brad. She managed through that investigation."

It was an unusual thing for Suzie to be nervous, and it plucked his nerves. In all the time they had been together, he had never seen her this way. One thing about Suzie: she always went after what she wanted with vigor. She wasn't afraid of anything. It's what attracted him to her in the first place. If it felt good—do it. That was her motto, and it worked for him.

"Trust me. She'll clam up. She's no good on her feet. Anyway, this is just the preliminaries," he said.

Brad and Suzie were waiting for Cynthia Steeple, their attorney, on the tall steps leading up to the law offices of Abercrombie and Abercrombie. The sun was shining, and it promised to be a warm day.

"I don't know how she can afford this place," Suzie said.

The sound of her insecurity annoyed him. Why couldn't she let up? Things were going just fine until she had that miscarriage six months ago.

"She probably has help from her mother. Anyway, this should be the last of it. I think they set this meeting up because they didn't want to go to court."

They had been round and round about why MacLeod had called this meeting.

Abby was already inside. Brad knew this because her car was parked outside. He wished Cynthia would show up. He liked her, too. Another one, not afraid of anything.

Cynthia pulled into the parking lot in a blue Jaguar, sleek with finely carved lines in contrast to its owner.

She was a short, curly-haired, blonde woman with the legs of a body builder, thick and wide. Her skirt was above the knee, her high-heeled shoes clicked on the cement steps, and she carried a small brief case.

"Hi, guys. Are you ready to take your daughter home?"

They shook hands all round.

"Yes." Suzie was emphatic. They walked together to the door. Brad held it open for both women.

The entrance hall was outfitted with a plush red carpet and a bank of elevators. The doors opened to a small room with one desk of a shiny dark wood, and seated behind it was a large woman of indeterminate age.

"May I help you?" she wheezed.

"Cynthia Steeple to see Douglas MacLeod."

"Have seat. I'll let him know that you're here."

She pointed to the sitting area with a sweep of one chunky arm. They took their seats on red leather cushions.

Chapter 40

Abby sat in a leather chair in the spartan office of Douglas MacLeod. Douglas looked like his brothers, but darker. His hair was nearly black instead of sandy red, but his eyes were brown. While his brothers were stocky and strong, he was slender and delicate. Duncan's hands were wide, calloused, and scarred. Douglas's were small and soft and manicured.

"They're here," Douglas said as he placed the phone back on its base.

Abby's stomach constricted.

Duncan reached over and took her hand. He nodded his head to say "Ready?" He sat in the chair next to her and looked as only a redhead could in a blue suit. She could stare at him all day.

"I'll just be glad when it's over."

"Let's go through to the conference room," Douglas said.

Abby followed Douglas, and Duncan followed Abby down the hall to the conference room. There was a large oval table in the middle of the room surrounded by chairs. On one wall was a sideboard complete with silver coffee urn. To the side of it was a silver tray laden with all the accessories for coffee or tea.

Duncan poured a cup a coffee and handed it to Abby.

"No, thanks. I'm fine." The hand she put up trembled slightly.

"It'll give you something to do with your hands," he said.

She took it from him and held the cup with both hands. The tremor made circles in the dark liquid. He poured himself a cup and they took seats on the far side of the table in front of the windows. Abby wished she could be on the other side. The windows would give her something to look at besides the sideboard during the uncomfortable meeting.

"I'll go get them." Douglas stepped out and closed the door behind him.

Duncan reached over and took Abby's hand. His was remarkably warm and steady. He smiled.

She squeezed his hand.

"I'm gonna be fine. I just hate confrontation, that's all."

"It's gonna be OK."

Duncan removed his hand when the doorknob turned. In walked Douglas followed by a curly-haired blonde with sunglasses perched on her head who looked like she boxed on the side. Brad and Suzie followed holding hands. Abby placed her cup carefully on the table and stood up. Cynthia Steeple put her briefcase on the table across from Duncan.

"I'm Cindy Steeple. You must be Abby." She reached across and handed Abby a few fingers to shake.

"And you are?" She speared Duncan with her gaze.

"A friend."

"I don't think we need any outsiders at this proceeding." She spoke to Douglas.

"He is a friend of Ms. Ericksen's, and he is here at her request."

Cindy Steeple flipped her hair around and received a nod from Brad.

"Very well, then as Mr. and Mrs. Ericksen seem to have no objection, we'll let it go."

Cynthia unzipped her case and pulled out a sheaf of papers. "Shall we sit down and get to business?"

Abby felt a cool calmness come over her. The fight was on.

"Quite frankly, Ms. Steeple, we were quite taken aback when we received your subpoena," said Douglas.

"Well, I don't know why you would be. Ms. Ericksen has refused repeatedly for the child's father to see the child."

"On the contrary, my understanding is that Mr. Ericksen has been in town and has made only two requests to see the child, for which"—Douglas looked down at his notes— "one was granted and the other denied due to illness in the child. There have been no further requests. Is that right?" He turned to Abby, and she nodded in the affirmative.

"Therefore, we propose to set up an agreement whereby both parents will have regular visitation."

"We might agree to that if the father has custody."

"On what grounds?"

"On the grounds that the father can offer the child much more than her mother can. He can afford to send the child to private school, pay for piano lessons—all that financial stability can supply. Mrs. Ericksen is a housewife and therefore will be home. It is commonly agreed that two parents in a household are the ideal situation for all children."

It was true. Brad did have more money than she had, but they would take Chloe over her dead body.

Brad was sitting silent next to Cynthia only occasionally agreeing with what a wonderful father he would be if only she would give up her Chloe. Suzie sat next to him gazing up at him in jubilation as though watching her champion win. Then Suzie turned her eyes to Abby. The cool triumph in them was too much. *Chloe would be better off with me*, Abby thought. She heard a car pull into the parking lot behind her. She glanced at Cindy. She had perched a set of golden half glasses on her nose and was reading from her yellow legal pad."...has also been investigated by Social Services." Cynthia was finished.

"The file on Ms. Ericksen has been closed. They have found no evidence of any wrongdoing on her part."

"We have talked to Julie." Duncan's voice startled all in the room. They all turned to look at him.

Suzie had blanched. The triumph was gone. She glanced at Brad nervously.

Cynthia looked at Brad. Brad shrugged.

"Who is that?"

"You'll have to ask your clients about that." Duncan said no more.

"If you'll excuse me, I'll speak to them outside."

The three of them got up and went into the hall.

"Perfect timing," Douglas said as he beamed at Duncan.

"Who's Julie?"

"Our trump card." Duncan smiled at Abby. "You know her as Ruth." Douglas looked back down at his notes; Duncan stood and went to the windows. Abby took a sip of her cold coffee. She heard a car drive away.

Chapter 41

"I think we should skip it and go home, Brad. She's so pathetic in there, all wide-eyed and everything."

"Who's Julie?" Cynthia asked.

"She's a friend of Suzie's, right, honey?" Brad answered.

"Yeah, she's been in trouble before, so I guess they think it will reflect badly on me or something, but I don't care, 'cause the minute I was in there, I thought we should just give it up anyways. She's so pathetic."

"Give it up?" Cynthia's voice was flat, reflecting that she was no longer fazed by anything.

Brad was glad to hear it. It was a little embarrassing to have to go back in there and back out, but at least he wasn't going to be saddled with the kid. *I wonder how Suzie would look with curly hair?* He thought to himself as he followed the women back into the conference room. Cynthia did not sit back down again.

"My clients have had a change of heart. They admit to no wrongdoing, but Mr. Ericksen doesn't have the heart to put his wife through a long custody battle. I'll have the papers to dismiss on your desk in the next couple of days."

Abby controlled her urge to jump up and down and holler "Yes!" She also controlled her urge to yell at Brad, as she had so many times before. *He doesn't have the heart to put Suzie through a custody battle?!*

"So now tell me about Ruth," Abby said to Duncan as they walked into Sammy's for lunch. Abby wasn't sure she could eat after all the excitement of the morning. Brad was gone. He wasn't going to sue for custody. He didn't even want to set up a regular visitation schedule.

"Ruth Julian Young Abercrombie."

The ramifications of what that meant ran through her mind. Did Suzie have the same problem as Ruth? "Was Suzie the woman that Ruth had alluded to?"

"Yep. Downtown Ruth has been running in the same circles as Suzie. Downtown Suzie calls herself Amber. Seems she has some interesting hobbies of her own that we figured she would rather keep secret."

"Oh, my goodness."

"Hey, girl!" Sharmagne led them to a table by the window.

"Ruth told me—the night that I had dinner with her—that she knew her friend Amber, Suzie, was involved in something desperate about a child.

When she realized it was you, she agreed to help."

"Now listen," Duncan said once they had gotten their food, "I have been instructed by my mother to find out if you will be attending the Easter on the Lawn party. You didn't RSVP."

"Oh, my gosh. I have been so caught up in— yes, I will come."

"Bring Chloe. I haven't seen her in a while."

"Well, you'll see her at church on Sunday since it's Easter."

Chapter 42

Easter morning was bright with new green leaves and clear yellow sunshine. The joy in the congregation of Bethel rivaled that at Christmas, for they came to celebrate the reason Christ came. He is risen. The men wore their finest suits, and the ladies were dressed in the palest colors of spring and summer.

Abby walked through the garden of worshipers holding Chloe with one hand and her dulcimer in the other. Duncan met them on the steps and took her dulcimer for her. Abby used her free hand to check her grandfather's tie pin at her throat and then took her seat on the altar. Chloe sat in between Debbie on the right and Duncan on her left. During the service, Abby saw Chloe rest her head on Duncan's chest as she herself had done that one night he had taken her to dinner. When it was time to stand, Chloe stuck up her hands to be lifted, and he picked her up.

Chapter 43

"One would put up with a lot to be mistress of Pemberley." The words from *Pride and Prejudice* echoed in her mind and caused her to giggle. She was out of her league, and it didn't matter what anybody said. The stately manor house of the MacLeod's rose out of the ground like a grand brick edifice worthy of Mr. Darcy and his Elizabeth. The effect would have been made perfect by the sight of ladies dressed in long, light-colored frocks from the nineteenth century. But the shorter ones worn this Easter did no harm to the illusion.

Erin MacLeod had pulled out all the stops, unless it was normal for the MacLeod's to have waiters walking around in white jackets with trays of food and drinks.

Abby was glad she had gone all out herself on Chloe's outfit. She was perfect in her little gown complete with gloves and hat. They walked up a cobblestone path to the house and were greeted by Erin herself.

"Abby, welcome." Erin was dressed in an

exquisite dress of muted gold. "This must be Chloe."

Abby followed Erin into the most beautiful house she had ever been in, but Duncan's home was more welcoming than regal. The colors were red and gold and blue and green. As they made their way to the terrace by way of a dark hallway, Abby saw on the wall a framed piece of old needlework. It was yellowed with age, but it still had good color although Abby suspected that the embroidery was more even when it was first done.

"It's beautiful," she said to Erin who stood behind her.

"It's the linen given to the first Duncan MacLeod."

"The song is real then."

"Of course it is. No one would ever make up such a ridiculous thing, although I will say that it has worked for this family. One thing the song leaves out. They only have six months from taking the oath to find a bride."

"Only six months."

"Duncan has only four months left." Erin turned and led her the rest of the way out.

She knew. Abby wasn't sure if Erin was giving her approval or not, but she definitely knew what Abby was up to.

Lord, give me courage, she prayed and put a hand to her throat. Chloe pulled on her hand, excited to get back outside.

From the terrace, the MacLeod men came into view. They were all dressed in their tartan. The other men were dressed in ordinary suits. Abby's eyes were drawn to Duncan. Chloe pulled on her hand. She wanted to be in the grass. Abby was glad this party was outside. All she had to do was follow Chloe around; there was no precious crystal for her to break.

As her eyes refocused to follow after Chloe, Abby noticed that she knew most everyone milling about on the lawn. Pastor Bob was there with his wife; Debbie and Kay shared the shade of a large maple tree with Angus; Rachel, Debbie's daughter, walked around and around the tree dragging her hand on its trunk. Pat Gordon was sitting on a bench near a bank of white azaleas in full bloom. Even Jack was there dressed in a suit that had grown bigger as he had grown older. His harmonica was sticking out of his breast pocket.

Duncan walked up to her trailing a smaller man dressed in a gray suit, who was followed by two women with wide-open faces.

"Abby." His voice thrilled her. "This is Max Gordon."

Max stuck out his hand. He looked like his father. Max introduced his fiancée, Maureen Mayhew, and her sister Grace.

"They are home on furlough."

Chloe pulled on Abby's hand. "Rachel–Momma–Rachel." She was pointing.

"Excuse me." She let Chloe pull her toward the tree.

"I don't want it, girl." Angus had laid down the law. Kay looked after him, mouth open, as he walked away toward Duncan and Max.

"What's going on?" Abby asked Debbie when Chloe was occupied with Rachel.

"All I did was tell him what we all think," Kay

began. "I was going to tell him at the grand opening, but I never had the chance. It was such a busy day. Anyway, here we all were, so I told him. Debbie is my witness. All I said was that we all thought that the business should go to him. That's all I said. Isn't that right, Debbie?"

"Yes, and he said that he didn't want it," Debbie replied.

"Well, I guess that settles that, doesn't it? Imagine that. Wait till I tell everybody. No one will believe it." Kay walked away toward Jack.

Abby and Debbie laughed together. They had talked to "everyone." The only die-hard fan of Angus MacLeod was Kay herself.

"This place is huge. I knew they were well off, but surely all this didn't come from a little charter boat business," Abby said.

"Oh, no. The Tours is only one of the businesses they own. They own the fishery, and most of the rest of the town—not to mention what they inherit."

"You're kidding. How did I miss that?"

"You've had your own things to worry about," Debbie said.

"That's the truth." Then the thought struck her that Bradley worked for the fishery. He must then work for Duncan. How could Duncan not have told her that? Anger surged. *How could he not have told her something like that?* She looked for him through the crowds of guests.

"Can I leave Chloe with you for a few minutes?"

"Of course you can..." Abby walked away without hearing the rest of the sentence.

"Duncan, may I speak to you alone?" she

whispered in a break in his conversation. He stopped and stood still to look at her.

"Of course. Follow me."

She followed him back into the house, back through the dark hallway, past the entrance to the kitchen, and into an immense room lined with bookshelves full of red and brown leather slashes. In the middle of the room sat a large mahogany desk. A couple of high-backed chairs were placed in front, for visitors, she guessed.

"What do you need?" he asked her once he closed the door. The windows of the room overlooked another vista of the Bay.

"Debbie just told me that you own the fishery and most of the rest of this town."

Duncan looked down.

"What is your question?"

"Bradley works for you, doesn't he? I want to make sure that you don't do anything stupid."

His eyes flashed up at her.

"I didn't mean *stupid*. I meant that I don't want you to send him away, fire him."

"Abby..." He smiled, stepped forward, and took her hands. "Bradley works for a contractor who works for me. I couldn't fire him even if I wanted to, besides which, I think Chloe needs a father too. I wouldn't send hers away."

Abby sank into one of the chairs behind her.

"I'm sorry. I shouldn't have assumed that you would do something like that."

"Well, you should know that he has put in for a transfer. He wants Colorado. If you want me to I could speak to Steve."

"No, he has to be free to make his own choices. Chloe will have to deal with it, but..."

"She'll be all right, Abby. He'll see to that." He pointed to the ceiling.

Her heart felt pounds lighter. He was right. God had not let them down yet. Once again Abby's hand went to her throat. She removed her grandfather's pin. She clasped it in her right hand and took a deep breath.

"Well, then, it's high time I speak to thee, Duncan MacLeod."

His eyes shot up at the reference to the old song. She took his hand. The blood rushed to her head and pounded in her ears. She slid down on her knee. He took both of her hands and pulled her to her feet.

"Get up."

"Duncan, I must do this right." He held onto her hands. His face was red, his eyes misty.

She tried to pull her right hand away, but he it held too tightly.

"Duncan."

He released her hand. She opened it to him.

"It isn't much. It was my grandfather's tie clasp. It only has a diamond chip." She blushed. "Except for Chloe, it is the most precious thing I have. I give it to you if you will have it and me as well."

He took the clasp from her hand and closed it in his fist. He dropped to his knees and closed her in his arms.

"I love you, Abby."

"I love you, Duncan."

This time he was not gentle. His kiss ignited the passion between them and caused them both to lose themselves in the bond that was growing in them and between them— love that would last a lifetime.

I hope you enjoyed meeting Duncan and Abby. If you did, won't you please take a moment to leave a review at your favorite retailer?

I hope to see you again soon for Angus's tale in **Finding Grace**.

During the meantime, you can find me on Facebook, on Twitter at @chevyhull and on my website, echull.com

Iz

63523474R00146

Made in the USA
Lexington, KY
09 May 2017